BY MOON

THE WITCHES OF PORTLAND, BOOK 5

T. THORN COYLE

BY MOON

In the light of the moon, secrets are revealed.

Darkness was good for a lot of the magic Selene was best at. Bindings. Uncrossings. Banishings. Oh, they could work the mechanics of prosperity or love spells, and of course collaborated with their coven on spells for justice, but...they were just more comfortable with working magic on the dark side of the moon.

That's a good thing, because poisonous magic is snaking through Selene's community, and things just got personal.

This is a standalone book in a linked series.
The main character uses they/them pronouns. This is not an editorial mistake.

1

SELENE

The scent of oil paint, turpentine, and linseed made Selene feel at home, chasing away the sense of unease they'd carried into the studio. The lights from the Morrison Bridge winked outside the chipped frames of the warehouse windows, lighting up the span and casting bright globes that sparkled on the waters of the Willamette.

The moon was almost full, and cast its own light across the dark ribbon of river.

The large studio space was quiet, the only sounds being the soft whoosh of cars heading toward the bridge, some laughter from the bar on the corner, and the tinny sound of music played too loud in someone's earbuds.

Only two other people were in the whole shared arts complex. People had better things to do at ten o'clock on a Friday night in June. It had been a hot day at the tail end of a scorching week, which meant the patio bars and outdoor cafés would be doing brisk business. Considering the sun didn't set until 9 p.m. at this time of year, and light faded later still, only a fool would be inside by choice.

Well, Selene was one of those fools. Happy to have

found a studio they could afford, and driven inside by the will to paint. And the need to escape that sinking feeling in the pit of their gut they'd been carrying around for the past few weeks.

Something was wrong, and Selene hadn't been able to pinpoint what. Oh, there was the backwash from the coven fighting off white supremacists the month before. The fallout from that was going to take time to settle, both in the coven and in the city itself. They'd won that battle but were under no illusions that they'd won the war.

And then Selene had to defend their thesis in order to graduate, which had been frankly harrowing. Because of a disagreement with their advisor, Selene almost didn't make it through.

After that, a person would think that Selene would take a break, but the opposite was true. Selene needed to prove to themself and their muse that art was paramount, grades and degrees or not.

Besides, art sometimes felt as if it was the only thing keeping Selene alive.

There had been way too much despair lately. Trans friends resorting to suicide to stop the hurting inflicted on them by a world that could not comprehend their beauty. Black boys murdered. Indigenous women missing. Hate crimes of all types on the rise. And Selene?

Selene was just a non-binary Goth femme, longing for love and not knowing where to find it. Or if they could even take the risk.

Love required too much exposure. Body and soul. That was the hardest thing about completing their thesis. Their advisor kept pushing Selene to dig deeper. To show more of themself.

That was how great art was made, Ms. Monroe said.

"You bare your soul to the canvas and paint it with your spit and blood."

Those stirring words sounded great in theory. But then Selene had to put them into practice and it really had about killed them. Exposing the inner landscape required vulnerability. And for an empath, vulnerability was always followed by the intrusion of other people's emotions. After the final thesis show and graduation ceremony they needed space. Selene only crawled out from the aerie of their attic home a week ago, anxious to get brush in hand again.

Luckily, Art Commons Collective had studio space available for non-members on a drop-in basis. Selene was trying it out, figuring they could always join in a month or two if they liked it. So far, they did.

The space was good, and the people seemed nice and left Selene alone, which was a good thing. Selene needed to ease into new social situations slowly.

Selene realized they'd been staring at the canvas, unseeing, for who knew how long. They sighed, then refocused on the still life taking shape. It was such a relief to paint something that, while it revealed something of the artist, didn't feel as if it were flaying them alive in the process.

So here Selene was, just post-graduation, with a fresh degree in graphic design, minor in fine art. Graphic design was interesting and paid the bills, and painting filled their soul.

The best paintings always drew them inside, working Selene like a perfectly executed magic spell, or a favorite song, thrumming through their body on a crowded dance floor.

But that was neither here nor there. Selene had this painting to complete. It was a challenging enough piece, an occult still life that attempted to convey the deeper mystery behind the objects gathered on the scarred walnut table. The deer skull. A black-handled knife. A spray of foxglove. And a chalice, painted as if it reflected a rising moon.

Limning a bright line along the edge of the deer's skull, Selene tried to tune in to the painting again. The moon was almost full. Selene could feel it. They had always been attuned to the moon. Their childhood fascination with the glowing orb was what led Selene to witchcraft, and, of course, to their name.

Selene, Goddess of the moon. Daughter of Titans, sister of the sun.

Selene had been raised by ordinary, flawed humans, and was an only child, but they felt as if they *could* be sibling to the sun. Maybe. Mostly, though, even though the full moon was gorgeous, Selene tucked themself away like the moon did behind the perpetually cloudy Portland skies.

Besides, darkness was good for a lot of the magic it turned out Selene was best at. Bindings. Uncrossings. Banishings. Oh, they could work the mechanics of prosperity or love spells, and of course collaborated with their coven on spells for justice, but...they were just more comfortable with working magic on the dark side of the moon.

Cassiel would give Selene shit if she knew her coven mate wasn't comfortable doing magic for themself. Not after Selene had given Cassie a hard time for not asking the Gods for help with her own little situation last winter.

They rubbed a long hand across their forehead, careful not to smudge any paint on their skin. Selene spent too much time on their makeup to mar it with the thick paint that slicked the horsehair brush.

Arrow and Crescent coven was a good fit for a witch dedicated to the moon. Coven members all had different deity affiliations, but the coven itself was dedicated to Diana, another Goddess with ties to the moon.

It was funny—gazing at the moon always grounded Selene more firmly on earth. It reminded them that they were on a rock in the middle of space, and that the rock was home. Just like Portland was, and likely always would be, home.

They stepped back from the painting a moment, trying to see the whole. The bright edge of the skull reflected the moon in the water. The blade edge needed drawing out to form a magic triangle created by the lines of light. A triangle of edges.

Just like Selene.

Sometimes it really felt as if they were nothing but edge. No center. No core. No soft, beating heart. No warm lips. No laughter.

It was as if Selene had been built to be a weapon. A sharp sword to be wielded against those who intended harm.

It wasn't a good feeling. Never had been.

Selene was a sharp sickle, not the lush fullness of the moon that practically set their long, dark hair afloat around their head.

"Fuck. May as well pack it in for the night," they murmured. Once this mood hit, there was nothing to do but drink or dance, have sex or sleep. No way were they ready for bed, and sex? Yeah, unless it was with Selene's own hand, that wasn't happening. It had been too long since they'd found someone interesting enough who was also interested in them.

"Drink and dance it is, then," Selene said. Setting the brush in the soaking jar, they began to scrape the paint off their palette. "I just hope you know what you're up to, moon."

Selene felt the small hairs on their arms stand up, as if something had just walked over their grave. They whipped their head around, looking for danger. Nothing. Selene's dark eyes rested on the still life. The water in the chalice on the table moved, rippling for a moment, as though a form attempted to take shape.

A trick of the eye? Or a message to pay attention? All Selene knew was, the studio didn't feel so homey anymore.

"Okay, Goddess. I'm listening. Just let me know what to do."

But please, don't make me be a knife right now. And don't expose me too much. I really need a break.

2

JOSHUA

Gods, the day had sucked. The Road Home was usually a haven, but the heat had made everyone fractious. One customer had been actually rude. Joshua had finally called it quits, closed the store early, and gone home to take a cool shower.

Now he was in his other home-away-from-home, sipping a mediocre cabernet, willing the wine to do its work. He really needed to relax, and usually Talisman was just the place to do it. Bass shook his legs in rhythm. *Untz, untz, untz...* The dark walls of the nightclub practically vibrated with it. The song was by some German Industrial band popular a decade ago. Joshua couldn't recall the name.

The club was filling up, finally. Joshua faced the door, which swung open with greater frequency, bringing in Rivetheads and Goths and the usual underdressed Port-landers who thought black T-shirts and jeans were sufficient for an evening out. Joshua, ever the dandy, wished people put in more effort, strictly for his own enjoyment.

He and Legis, a strapping brute of a redheaded Thelemite, were ensconced in one of the padded booths on the edge of the dance floor, enjoying the view. There were a few particularly well-turned-out boys and girls in corsets, leather, and full makeup. All were easy on the eyes.

"When are you going to ditch the goatee, man?" Legis said.

"The day you decide to start wearing backward ball caps."

Legis snorted and drank more beer.

Usually, Joshua would be prowling, striking up flirtations with one of the many women he'd already dallied with, or one of those he hadn't done that particular dance with yet. On occasion, there was even a man that caught his fancy.

Tonight? The thought of it just made him tired. He was off his game, and not sure why. Fuck it. Might as well drink and talk magic with his friend.

Magical sigils glowed from the ceiling and walls. Nothing to summon any real angels or demons, or any of the ancient powers, thank every God and Goddess. No, these sigils were strictly out of someone's dark fantasy of what talismanic sigils *should* look like.

Club goers summoned enough with their drinking and dancing, flirting and fighting, without having actual symbols bringing who knew what into being.

Although, come to think of it...

"You ever think these fake sigils are actually summoning something?" he asked.

Legis looked around, running a hand through his short red hair. As magicians went, he was a good guy. He had started following the works of Aleister Crowley when he was a teen, attracted by the whole "wickedest man in the world" hype. Fifteen years later, he was still a member of the

OTO—the Ordo Templi Orientis, Crowley's magical lodge —having stayed for the deep spiritual practice.

Joshua hung out with Legis because not only was he smart, and a good magician, he was one of the Thelemites that did *not* act as if working his will in the world gave him license to be an asshole.

"I don't know, man," Legis replied. "There's certainly enough juice raised in here on a regular basis to summon any damn thing. It's why I always bring extra protection out clubbing."

Legis gestured to a chunk of obsidian bounded in silver. The amulet rested just under his unicursal hexagram, the angular knot that revealed a six-pointed star for those who knew what they were looking at.

"I hope you've got some condoms to back up that obsidian," Joshua quipped.

"Asshole," Legis replied, a rakish grin slicing across his broad features. He took a deep swallow of his lager. "As if you're one to talk. But seriously, I've seen people summon all sorts of shit without meaning to. It happens all the time. I swear that half of the drug casualties we see in the clinic are compounded by hallucinations of things that sometimes feel a little too real, magic-wise."

"Damn. You've never told me that. You know, I used to think that people who weren't willing to put in the training to do magic properly had their own weird protections. You know, that they couldn't summon anything if they tried, because they didn't have the will." He paused to drink more wine, stroking a hand across the stubble on his chin. "But I've seen enough in the past year to show me that people get caught in the crossfire, for one thing, and that other people get taken advantage of by entities tapping into their mental imbalances."

"Ain't that the truth."

Both men retreated for a moment, seeking contemplation through fermented grape and grain. Joshua wondered what it would take to up his own magical game again. Member of no lodge or society, he'd always skirted around the edges. Oh, he knew plenty. He was a tarot and astrology master, and he'd worked his own spells, conjuring up The Road Home, for one thing. But if he was honest?

His shop catered to folks seeking escapism as much he served people seeking themselves, or something larger than themselves.

"What do you think about people who just seem to want to run away?" Joshua asked.

Legis shrugged. "I don't think about them much anymore. They used to bother me. Worry me, even. But now I figure that everyone has their own pain and damage, and we all just find out how to best deal, you know?"

Damn it. Too close to home. Joshua's meditation practice had slacked off over the past year, as had his studies. Oh, he still worked the small magics, and had helped out Arrow and Crescent coven when needed, but part of him knew he was skating the surface lately. And it was because of what Legis just mentioned. He was avoiding his pain and damage. Not really dealing at all.

"What's *your* regular practice?" he asked Legis. "The daily stuff, I mean."

Legis set his pint down on the table. "Regulated breathing. Silent meditation, which is really just more breath work, right? And I do the LBRP every day."

"Really?"

The Lesser Banishing Ritual of the Pentagram was a ceremonial cleansing rite, filled with intonations of sacred letters, gestures to each direction, and required the magician to call upon angels and the ineffable name of God. Simple, right?

"It's the best practice I know to keep my space clear and keep myself centered. If I don't do that every day, shit starts to creep in, you know?"

Joshua did know. His life had felt clean and centered once upon a time. He'd let the creep happen, though, that much was clear. His shop was steadily losing sales. His sex antics had grown less and less interesting. And he'd started relying a bit too heavily on the wine.

Shoving his wine away, he focused his dark brown eyes on Legis's green ones.

"I need to start again, man. I..." He wished he had some water but didn't want to break the moment by going to the cooler at the bar. His long fingers tapped at the wooden table. Legis just waited, calmly drinking his beer as though Joshua wasn't sweating across the booth from him.

Joshua was about to break the cardinal rule of friendship between men. You either started out sharing shit or you kept it theoretical. They'd always been theoretical. Talking magical technique. Women. Music. Catching the occasional film. Never talking about the effects of any of them.

He took in a deep breath.

"Things aren't going right anymore. All the little shit is falling apart. Nothing big, but...that slow creep you were talking about."

"Things are out of true."

"Yes! That's it...like everything's gone a little wobbly."

"You have to find your core again, Joshua. Frankly, I've been watching it for a while, the way you've wandered off from yourself. Like you said, it's nothing big, and you clearly still have juice, which is why I haven't said anything. But...yeah."

"So what do I do?" he said.

"You start back at the beginning. That's what we all do, man. What's your first practice?"

The door swung open, and the most gorgeous Goth in the world stepped through. A long sweep of black hair, pressed straight. Dark liner around dark eyes. Pale, pale skin. Ruby lips. Silver jewelry winking from a black, flowing shirt. Tall. So tall. Natural height only accented by the patent leather platform buckle boots.

Joshua half rose from the booth, then sank back down. Legis quirked an eyebrow his way, before turning to see who or what had caused Joshua's reaction.

Legis grinned.

"Don't say a word," Joshua warned.

"Me? I'm just drinking my beer, minding my business. But you've got it bad, boy."

Joshua slid his wine glass back across the table, and took a hefty drink.

Selene.

Damn it all. Selene was here.

3

———

SELENE

At around 11:30, the club was pretty full. Selene stood just inside the door, clutching at their little fake-leather bat purse, having left their usual heavy messenger bag in the trunk of the old Toyota parked two blocks away. If it weren't for the platform boots they'd changed into, Selene could have walked from the studio, that was how close it was.

Come to think of it, the club was pretty close to the soup kitchen Aiden worked at, too. Maybe Selene could start volunteering there, now that school was off the schedule.

The smell of beer, wine, and amber oil touched to swan-like throats hovered in the air. It helped relax Selene. At least, one part of them relaxed. The familiarity of the music, the darkness, the swirl of colored lights, fake fog, and people helped calm down the animal part that always wanted to run.

Being an empath was a bitch. Despite years of training to ground and filter out other people's emotions, when other people were in a group, it was too easy for things to leak through.

The room was filled mostly with the usual white Portland Goth and Industrial crew, sprinkled with a few Black, Asian, and Latinx faces. Oh, there was racism in the Goth scene, just like anywhere, but mostly, the freaks banded fiercely together, protecting their own.

The main fights Goths had were with each other, over sex, broken hearts, or sometimes, on rare occasions, drugs.

So yeah, Talisman felt good to Selene's soul. It felt like a place they could be, as they were. A six-foot-tall-in-heels, non-binary, Goth, femme witch.

Selene reached for their spiritual practices, slowing their breathing and wiggling toes encased in the stompy platform boots.

Looking at the black-painted wood planks beneath their boots, Selene exhaled, imagining the breath flowing all the way to the edges of their skin. It helped. They relaxed a little more, then sent a second slow breath out toward the shining edge of their aura, reinforcing their personal boundary. Better. Should've remembered to do that *before* entering the club.

And, finally, they looked up.

There he was, staring with a look they couldn't quite place. A good look? A bad look? Joshua seemed a bit flustered, which seemed unlike him. His hair was even slightly dented from where his top hat had rested. The hat was now on the table beside him.

He flashed a small half-smile, quickly gone.

Then the person with him turned. Legis. Selene relaxed a bit more. They liked the big magician. He was good people. Made them feel safe, actually.

And Joshua? Selene liked him, but he always left them feeling a bit unsettled. Wanting to move forward and backward simultaneously. Like right now. Something in him pulled at Selene like the moon.

Selene didn't trust that attraction for a minute. They never did.

But frankly, Legis and Joshua were the two people in the club that Selene was closest to, so they pointed their boots toward the booth where the two men were now quietly drinking and talking, hunched toward each other.

That in itself was a little weird. Usually one of them would have waved Selene over. Oh well, any port in a storm, right?

They wove through clusters of two and three, skirting the edges of the teeming dance floor. They would hit the bar first.

"Hey Selene!" Janice teetered on blood red heels, already half-drunk. Seal-brown hair fell in thick waves to her creamy bare shoulders. Sweat marred her perfectly made-up face.

That was strange, considering they were standing beneath a huge whirring fan blasting air toward the dance floor.

"Hey Janice. You doing all right?"

"Right as rain," the woman said, before staggering off, tugging at her black dress, adjusting it around her hips. Selene looked after her, brow creasing in concern. Janice wasn't usually a heavy drinker. Selene wondered what was wrong.

Space cleared up at the small bar. It reminded Selene of a bar in someone's basement. No stools, just a countertop long enough for four people to stand and order, and then move out of the way. This was a transactional space, not a place to stay and drink.

Laughter cracked across the room. Janice again, having

shoved herself into a booth between two men. Damn it. Selene hoped the men wouldn't take advantage of Janice. Currently, the two were looking on with amusement. Selene hoped things stayed that way.

"What can I get you, gorgeous?" Becca was running the bar tonight. A white woman whose curves were so extreme her tight jeans couldn't encase them. Beneath her vintage Fields of the Nephilim tour T-shirt, a lush roll of fat hovered above the '90s studded belt encircling Becca's hips, tapering up toward a solid waist before curving back out to her breasts.

Becca's body was a feat of natural engineering that Selene sometimes envied, their own slim, lanky form seeming pedestrian in comparison.

"Gin martini, please." Selene leaned on the bar top, watching Becca measure out the gin and vermouth, ice the stemmed glass, dump ice into the metal shaker. One of the nice touches Talisman insisted on was still serving wine, cocktails, and beer in proper glasses. There was surprisingly little breakage, and it catered to the Gothic romance angle far better than plastic.

So, it was good for business, as well as the environment. The owner, Roderick, was nothing if not practical.

"Hey Becca, do you know what's up with Janice?"

Becca strained the cold liquid into the chilled glass and shook her head.

"No clue. She only had one glass of merlot, as far as I can tell."

That wasn't good at all. If it wasn't alcohol, it was drugs. Didn't seem like Rohypnol to Selene, but they were no expert on that, either. Though they had been roofied once.

Becca slipped three green olives into the glass and set it on the bar just as Selene slid a card across.

Becca shook her head. "On the house tonight."

"Really?"

"Got to keep the regular crew happy, right? Roderick wants to up the fancy quotient—too many dressed down folks these days—and you're one of the fanciest people I know."

Selene fished a few dollar bills from the little bat bag and smoothed them onto the bar top.

"Thanks," they said, but Becca had already turned to the next patron.

Taking a sip of the too-full drink, Selene set her gaze on Joshua and Legis's booth. Good, they were still there, and no one else had joined them.

Selene angled their tall body and skirted their way back through the crowd. The music shifted to Covenant, the bright electronic pulse underpinning Eskil's soaring vocals. Selene smiled.

"Selene." Joshua's voice was sober.

"Please, join us. Help me tell this jackass he needs to up his game," Legis said, scooting over.

Selene was relieved to sit next to Legis instead of Joshua. He was easygoing and never treated them like anything other than a respected sibling. Joshua, however? Gah.

Of course, sitting across from the man was barely any better.

There it was, nervous sweat under their arms. Hopefully it wouldn't spread. Selene didn't want to have to do makeup repair.

Keep breathing, Selene.

Joshua was no-go-land for Selene. A nice guy, and he'd helped out the coven in the past, but he was also a known player.

Not that there was anything wrong with that. Selene

knew both committed polyamorous people and folks who just enjoyed sleeping around.

Selene had just never been a casual-sex sort of person. As a matter of fact, they vacillated between hot crushes and feeling completely shut down. They'd checked in with their coven mentors about it, and both Brenda and Raquel said that it was likely a side effect of their particular empathic psychic skills.

"Once you learn to trust the ways your spiritual practices work for you, hopefully you won't feel the need to shut down like that." Raquel had said that a year ago, and Selene was definitely getting more adept at managing emotionally charged situations. But clearly being around a hot guy still felt flustering.

They took another swallow of the perfect martini. It was crisp and cold, with just enough vermouth to temper the gin. Selene forced themself to slow down and sip the drink, the way it deserved. Drinking too fast. Another sign that Joshua was making them nervous. They set the stemmed glass back down on the table.

Like all the witches in Arrow and Crescent, Selene drank, sure, but never a lot. Red wine was usually their beverage of choice. Selene wasn't sure what made them order a martini tonight.

And why did it even matter?

Maybe they didn't want to be drinking the same thing Joshua was. Not raising the same burgundy liquid to stain their lips. As if his wine was their wine.

Oh, cut it out. Selene gave themself an internal eyeroll and a small shake. Their hand shot out, and the martini tipped. Legis grabbed at it, but too late. Cold gin spilled across the table, cascading in a rush over the side, straight onto Joshua's trousers.

He leapt up, batting at the liquid with a tiny cocktail napkin.

Damn it, Selene. You big dork.

Then he started to laugh. Legis joined in. Selene rose, humiliated, cheeks burning.

"I'm so sorry!" they said. "Let me…"

Face still burning, Selene turned and shoved their way toward the bar, Joshua's voice trailing after them over the thump and surge of the music.

"Selene! It's okay…"

It wasn't okay. It was never okay. The body betrayed them, every damn time.

Anything Selene wanted badly, their body acted this way. It was as if their subconscious was trying to bust through the wall of protection, reaching for the desired object. It was this way with everything except painting, whether pixels or oil. And coven. Thank Goddess for the coven.

They stopped stock still at the far edge of the bar. Becca looked up. "Everything okay?"

"I'm a dork and spilled my drink. Glass didn't break, though."

"No problem," Becca said, grabbing a white bar rag from beneath the counter. "Here. Make you another?"

Selene shook their head. "No. Thanks. A glass of pinot noir, maybe?"

As if wine would be any better. Nothing was going to make Selene sophisticated around Joshua, that was for sure. Except maybe a personality transplant. Their body was a traitor to their emotions. Or maybe it was the other way around.

Someone crashed into Selene from behind, shoving them into the bar. Selene's hand smacked out to catch themself, barely missing the glass of wine Becca had just set down.

"Hey!" Becca shouted. "Watch out, dickhead!"

Selene pushed back from the bar and slowly turned.

"Sorry, man. I mean, lady. I'm…"

The man was small and thin. He was starting to shake. Selene grabbed his shoulders. His arms trembled and vibrated under their hands. He felt warm.

"My heart…" he slurred out. "I'm flying, man. Flying."

Then he dropped to the ground and began to seize.

"Becca?" Selene whirled toward the bartender.

"On it!" Becca already had a phone to her ear, calling 911. Then Legis was at Selene's side, shouting into their ear. They sensed Joshua somewhere just behind him.

"We need to get this guy rolled onto his side!"

Becca thrust some bar towels at Selene, who stared at them for a moment, not understanding. Then motion clicked in again.

They shoved the folded towels between Legis's big hand, which cradled the man's head, and the hard floor.

What in Goddess's name was going on?

4

JOSHUA

Finally home from the club, having helped get the seizing man safely into an ambulance, Joshua felt hyped up and exhausted all at once. Too keyed up to sleep, too tired to read, he wasn't in the mood for a movie or television.

He looked around his tidy living room, past the long, green velvet couch and the two comfy damask-covered chairs. His eyes raked over the gold-framed print of poisonous herbs hanging on the wall, flanked by old woodcuts in simple burgundy rectangles. Scanned the low bookcases the bordered two walls. Books, of course. Mostly on magic, but two of the cases held some favorite fiction. On top were candlesticks stuffed with beeswax tapers. A ceramic human skull, with a jade plant growing out of the crown.

Two metal, art deco lamps with jadeite rings and green lampshades, coupled with a brass floor lamp, cast a warm light over it all.

"Goth as fuck," he commented, suddenly tired of himself. Of his life.

The night's events had him shaken. First of all, there was Selene. No one affected him the way she did. *They* did. He had trouble remembering the correct pronoun. Selene was so femme, it was hard sometimes to remember they were non-binary. It was their femme qualities that hit him so hard. Coupled with the wicked-interesting thoughts he could see flashing behind their eyes, right before they froze and clammed up.

Figured. The one person he was interested in for more than a night or three didn't like him and Joshua couldn't figure out why.

But that was the least of it. Then that guy collapsed on the ground and started seizing. Joshua was one of five people who called for an ambulance. Legis, Becca, and Selene got the guy rolled onto his side with folded-up bar towels beneath his head.

Something about the man seemed strange. Off. Joshua had seen people seizing before. This was something else. He, Legis, and Selene had stayed until the ambulance carted the poor guy away. Then they'd all begged off, and gone their separate ways.

For some reason, the whole thing felt too troubling to hash out over drinks and they all knew it. So here he was, alone in his tiny nineteenth-century pyramid-roofed bungalow bought a few years before during a real estate dip when The Road Home had been doing particularly well.

It was beautiful, his Goth-as-fuck home, and he couldn't imagine living any other way. Joshua honored life by honoring death, but there was one death in particular that still haunted him.

It was just the sort of home he and Jessie had dreamed about. The one they were going to find, and refurbish, and paint, and then gather a gorgeous mix of medieval- and Victorian-looking objets d'art to fill it.

Before she was killed by some asshole drunk going too fast the wrong way down a one-way street. Once the drunk figured it out, he tried to course correct by pulling a U-turn onto the sidewalk. He had survived.

Jessie had lingered for six hours before succumbing to the sweet, dark kiss.

"Buck up," he muttered to himself, before heading to the kitchen for a glass of water. The kitchen was compact and efficient and Joshua's one concession to the twenty-first century was seen here. A red SMEG refrigerator with classic lines and a human-sized scale. Red stove. Red microwave on the black granite countertop. Black, reflective cabinets. Concrete sink and polished, wide plank fir floors, stained as dark as they would go.

He pulled a vintage black drinking horn pedestal glass from a cabinet and ran the water until it was cold, gulping it down as if his life depended on it.

He supposed it did.

Setting the glass down with a clink, he leaned back against the counter and stared through the squared-off kitchen lintel, through the conjoined dining and living rooms. The kitchen was an addition, along with the bathroom. The original home was four rooms. Two small bedrooms, a living room, and the kitchen, with an outhouse in the back yard. Somewhere in the early 1920s or 1930s, someone had added the small addition to the back, extending the home out from its original square.

It suited Joshua. It would have suited Joshua and Jessie better. It worked fine to host the revolving parade of women that Joshua took home, treated with deep respect, and then let go.

But he was tired of that. Itching for something more.

So what're you going to do now? He could feel the question, practically hanging in the air. The eternal question, it had cropped up a lot in recent days, and dovetailed right back into his conversation with Legis about magical practice. What was Joshua's basic practice?

It used to be meditation and pendulum work. Breath work. These days? He did the occasional Tarot or astrology reading. He burned incense in the shop every day before opening.

But deeper magic? Other than some recent stuff with Arrow and Crescent Coven, he didn't do it anymore. And solid daily practice had slipped away...when? Six months ago?

His subconscious must have been signaling his coming dissatisfaction.

"So do something about it," he said, and walked back into the living room to the wooden cigar box that held his favorite Tarot deck.

Well, *favorite* was too strong a word, as there were decks whose images struck his eye as more beautiful. *Preferred* reading deck was more like it.

It was the Thoth deck, painted by Lady Frieda Harris based on the instructions of Aleister Crowley. Legis's main man.

As he unwrapped the deck from the swathe of blue silk and began to shuffle the cards, Joshua wondered. Maybe he should go talk with Frater Louis, current head of Legis's lodge. Take a Zero Degree, the first initiation required for membership. Start doing the basic rituals and practices. See what happened.

He respected Louis and Legis, but had always found the

OTO a bit much. But he needed something, that was for sure, and ceremonial work resonated more clearly with him than witchcraft or anything else.

"Show me what I need to know. What do I need to pay attention to right now?"

The cards *shushed* between his hands, slipping through his fingers. He strolled back into the dining room, hooking a boot around one of the curved-back dining chairs and sitting down at the polished walnut table. The cards cracked and snapped against the wood. He shuffled them another six times, then stopped, took a breath, and cut the deck into three piles.

Joshua focused his attention more deeply and opened his awareness to the cards. The stack in the middle seemed to vibrate, so he picked it up and stacked the other two piles beneath it.

"Show me what I need to know," he repeated, then turned three cards over onto the dark wood. The brass deco-style chandelier lit up the cards, a brighter light than he usually preferred.

Joshua usually did readings by candlelight, but after tonight? He wanted as much illumination as possible. He didn't even know why.

First card. The Lovers. Gemini. The Black and white child. The king and the queen. All overlooked by the benevolent figure, who brings them together. Synthesis. The alchemical wedding.

Okay.

Second card. The Devil. Capricorn. Vitality and life force. Lust and creativity, yearning to be harnessed and set free.

Third card. The Moon. Pisces. The threshold of renewal.

All the things held in darkness, clawing their way toward the light. As Crowley himself wrote, the Moon was "the poisoned darkness which is the condition of the rebirth of light."

Something needed to be reborn, that was clear. But was this message just for him? It didn't feel like it, but that was the simplest place to start.

How was he supposed to interpret these? The alchemical wedding the Lovers card pointed to required a lot of concerted effort. The alchemist had to dissolve themselves and resolve themselves again in order to bring about the new form. The true form of their spirit. So, if nothing else, that pointed to Joshua renewing his practice and getting serious about his inner work again. The outer work and the inner needed to happen simultaneously.

Huh. Maybe that was part of the issue with The Road Home. He hadn't been paying enough attention to his inner life lately, so the outer was running off the rails.

The Devil. Life force. He sure as hell wasn't harnessing that lately, either. He'd stopped having sex with random club goers a few weeks ago because he was finding it exhausting. Depleting. Joshua had no idea what would feed his life force, but at least he knew to look for it now.

As with any magical operation, awareness was the key. He just hadn't been paying enough attention lately.

Which left the Moon. All the things that lived in the waters of the subconscious, rising toward the light of moon. The dark night of the soul. Entering the depths of self in order to know.

The thought terrified Joshua. What if he didn't *want* to know? What if avoiding that knowledge was the only thing keeping him sane?

And if this reading wasn't about him at all? That message was going to take some work to figure out.

He took another deep breath, then rose, heading to the living room for the notebook and pen that lived in the cigar box.

He had to get this reading down on paper.

5

SELENE

The Inner Eye reflected the morning sun, catching the light and throwing it back in a rainbow of color refracted from crystals and stained glass. Brenda always kept the windows of her esoteric shop blindingly clean, hiring day laborers to clean them once a week, rain or shine.

The shop opened at ten, and it was just past that, so Selene hoped to catch Brenda before things got busy.

Selene eyed the windows, almost at the front door, when a sudden shiver gripped them. Concurrent waves of vertigo and nausea swept through their body.

What the hell?

Selene slammed the glass door open and ran through display cases of crystals and Tarot cards, past the book area, toward the hanging Celtic-knot-patterned curtain that led to the back of the shop.

Cold sweat slicked over their skin. Selene just hoped to make it to the toilet.

"Selene!" Tempest called out. Her sweep of hair was a fading purple this week. Selene just waved a hand and dove past the curtain, bumping into Brenda, who was just coming back out onto the shop floor.

"Are you okay?" Brenda asked.

"Not now!" Selene was barely going to make it. They slammed open the door to the WC, flipped the lid up, and fell, hard, to their knees. Selene barely got their long hair back before the heaving began.

Their body racked with flaring chills and heat, convulsing until the piece of toast and coffee that had been their breakfast wasn't inside anymore. Then they heaved some more, stomach cramping until all that was left was spit.

Selene pushed away from the bowl a few inches, dimly aware of splashing sounds. Brenda.

"Here. Let me help you."

Brenda ran a cool, damp cloth over Selene's face. There went the makeup. Oh well, Selene had probably sweated through most of it, anyway.

"Up," they said. "Please?"

Brenda helped Selene to stand and turned them toward the wash basin. Selene made the mistake of looking in the mirror. Yep. They looked like shit. Mascara running down pale cheeks. Foundation streaked from tears and the washcloth.

"May I have that?" Selene asked.

Brenda handed them the washcloth. Selene ran it under cold water that felt so good they could have stood there all day, letting it rush over their hands. Instead, they wet the cloth again and finished the job Brenda had started.

"Are you sick?" their coven mate asked. Brenda and her best friend, Raquel, were co-founders of Arrow and Crescent Coven. They'd both taught Selene, who had already surpassed the two women in some areas of magic. But Selene still had a lot to learn in others. And in life.

Selene looked up, seeing their friend in the mirror, worried creases marring her peachy forehead. Dark brown hair coiled in tendrils around Brenda's sweet face. Laugh lines marked the corners of her blue eyes, and deep runnels were just starting at the edges of her mouth. If middle age looked that good, Selene figured it wouldn't be so bad.

If they made it that far.

Selene wrung the washcloth out and draped it over the edge of the sink.

"I don't know. I wasn't, but then I all of a sudden was. But…"

"But what? Come on out into the meeting room. I'll make you a cup of tea."

Selene followed her into the large room used as a classroom and meeting space, as well as a break room for staff. Banners representing the four elements of air, fire, water, and earth hung from each of the four walls. Brenda steered Selene to one of the few chairs with cushions in the room, and gave a gentle shove. Selene was only too happy to acquiesce.

Brenda stepped toward the tiny kitchen area, loose black trousers swaying around her long legs beneath a pale blue tunic top. A moonstone glowed over her breastbone as usual. She filled the kettle and rooted through the tea drawer for some herbs.

Selene wracked their brain, trying to figure out what had happened. They felt weak now, but fine.

It was that damn ghost walking over their grave again. Just like last night in the studio. But today was stronger.

Brenda came over with a steaming cup smelling of fresh

mint. Selene's shoulders relaxed, and they held out their hands.

"Careful. Hot."

Brenda sat down next to her, and placed a hand on Selene's arm.

"Ready to talk about it?"

Sudden tears pricked at the corners of Selene's eyes. This was so weird. What the hell was happening? Was it a psychic attack? Or something else?

"Sometimes being an empath sucks. It's...there's something strange going on, and I don't think it's just me. I mean, some of it's me. But..." Selene shook their head, and blew across the surface of the pale yellow-green tisane, buying time. "Twice now, I've felt a something strange pass over me, and today it made me puke. And then last night at the club, people were acting strange. And I've been getting a backwash of emotion from it all and haven't been able to block it out. Not like usual."

"Acting strange how?"

Selene sipped at the tea. It was soothing. Comforting.

"One woman acted like she was totally wasted, but the bartender said she'd only had one drink. And then this man ended up having seizures. Got rushed to the hospital."

"Did it seem like they were drugged?"

Selene looked at Brenda, whose usually serene face was creased with concern.

"They felt *wrong,* Brenda. Maybe they were drugged. I think probably so. But it felt worse than that."

"Like magic?"

Selene thought about it. Rolled the idea around their head.

"Yes."

"What kind of magic? Could you trace it if you had to?"

Selene took a shaky breath in, tried to drop into their center. See what they could see.

Hot and cold flashed along the edges of their skin. They shoved the cup of tea at Brenda and ran for the toilet, barely making it before the heaving started up again.

Goddess, what is happening to me?

6

JOSHUA

Last night's events still running in his head, Joshua hopped off the bus and walked the two blocks to The Road Home, black leather purse banging at one hip. At ten-thirty, the morning was already warm, and he was thankful he'd left the top hat at home and worn linen trousers today. Thankful for the shade from the trees and buildings, too.

Shopkeepers swept sidewalks, getting ready to haul out racks of clothing or sale books. The coffee shops were doing brisk business.

Scents from the bagel shop were tempting, but for now, he had coffee in an insulated mug and he felt the need to get into his store and make sure no disasters loomed before his noon opening time.

He really felt as if a sword hung over his head, and the reading wasn't helping. On the surface, that combination of cards could either look terrible, good, or not-so-bad. It all depended on context and interpretation.

If it was just a reading about himself, okay. Yeah. Joshua got it. He'd been avoiding the deep personal work—

wrestling the demons brought on by Jessie's death—for years. And as a consequence, all the little things feeling off lately could be the product of that. Eventually, a person became so knotted up inside that anything they attempted to do could become twisted, too.

Maybe that's all it was. *Probably* that's all it was.

But then there were the weird events at the club. Selene acting so strangely, spilling their drink. Barely looking at him. Janice getting drunk. And that guy, collapsing and seizing. It all felt strange. He wished he'd paid better attention to it all now, but frankly, Joshua been too fixated on Selene and on his conversation with Legis to notice much.

He turned the corner and smiled as he saw his shop, ensconced one block off the main drag on a street teeming with maples, ginkgoes, and tulip trees. A sushi restaurant was across the street, and beyond that were the foursquare and Craftsman homes Joshua loved. Built for families, they were grander than his little bungalow, but of a similar feel. They'd all been built around the same time. Early 1900s, barely post-Victorian.

The orange door of The Road Home beckoned. As he approached it, he saw a package on the stoop. Funny. He had no current shipments due, and besides, none of his distributors would leave a package like that. They knew to deliver during business hours, when he or his employees were there to sign.

The cardboard box was around six by four inches. Joshua set down his leather purse and travel coffee mug, and squatted over the box to examine the label. *Alchemical Curiosities* it read, in an elaborate cursive font. Underneath it was a Portland PO Box instead of a street address. The "to" label was computer generated and printed.

Joshua looked around to make sure no one was close enough to notice anything strange, took a breath and held one hand over the box. Fingers splayed outward, he tried to remember what it was like to sense the energetic signature of a thing.

A practice that used to be so basic to him. One he'd done every day when first clinging to magic as a thing that might save him after Jessie's death.

Hoping magic might offer him a way to communicate with her spirit.

It hadn't done that, but it had offered him a chance to build the life he now had. That was good for a while. Very good. His heart had even eased after awhile.

There were no actual excuses for his current lax practice. Joshua had just allowed himself to come unmoored. It had felt too hard to keep things going on his own after the initial wracking pain and scramble to stay alive had passed. He'd needed his magic after Jessie was killed. Once life had normalized, he'd forgotten it was necessary to maintain.

And to stay fully engaged with life.

"You fool," he said, and closed his hand. He'd gotten nothing off it. No energy signature at all, just the feel of inert cardboard, wood too far removed from the growth of trees. Joshua picked up the box, hoisted his bag again, and unlocked the orange door and turned the old-fashioned brass knob.

Crossing the threshold, he walked past the waving ribbons of wishes people had hung from one of the elaborate "trees" inside the door, and inhaled the mélange of scents. His custom oil blends. The ghost of incense. The tuber roses he hadn't been able to resist buying the other day, now displayed in a large vase on the back counter.

He flipped the switches near the door, turning the lights on and activating the small fountain that burbled happily just to the right of the entrance. The sound greeted everyone who walked through the door, clearing their energy. It set the stage for an entrance into someplace special—just a little otherworldly—but familiar and comforting all the same.

The shop was still his favorite place in the world. Walking into it was like walking into an enchanted forest. The walls and ceiling were painted with a tall canopy of slender-trunked birches. Faeries made by a local artist flew here and there, guiding customers further in, past books, statuary, and on toward the display cases filled with amulets, gemstones, and finely crafted jewelry.

Joshua disarmed the alarm system and flicked on the lights. The display cases shone and gleamed, showing a few blank spots that he'd need to restock before opening.

He breathed a sigh of contentment. The shop was designed to be a haven for seekers of all types. For people who just wanted to escape a bad situation that had them feeling trapped, to those who needed comfort...the people he and Legis had talked about last night? Joshua had built a place for them. And, he now realized, he'd built a place for himself. For the parts of him that still ached and felt a little lost, despite the shining front he presented to the world.

Glamour. He still had that magic in spades. A good cravat and fancy waistcoat, coupled with the magic that he still possessed? It all still worked.

But it seemed that wasn't enough anymore.

Joshua wound his way to the back of the shop, which, being set on a corner, was brighter and more open than the warren out front, lit by a bank of windows with stained glass strips at the top. The windows opened up onto a quiet residential street.

The shop didn't only cater to those in need of a sense of wonder. There were deeper mysteries at play here, too, for those drawn to them, and also those who knew where to look. The back of the store held them all.

He had amulets to call fiery angels. Books to unlock secrets of the mind. Pendulums to offer guidance to those seeking to expand their awareness.

Yeah. Maybe he'd pick up a pendulum again. Maybe that could be his basic practice to start with, along with the meditation he'd skipped again this morning.

"If you're going to do this thing, you've got to adjust your schedule, man. Make a commitment."

He set the box down on a long wooden countertop designed specifically for the space. One of his workers polished the thing every month, so it always had a slight glow about it.

His coffee mug and square leather purse joined the box. Joshua rounded the counter, slid open a drawer and pulled out a box cutter.

Carefully slicing open the tape, he drew the cardboard flaps back.

Beneath a layer of bubble wrap was a handwritten note on heavy cream paper that said "Free samples! Enjoy!" Joshua lifted the note to reveal a row of two-ounce salve jars, labeled with the big, cursive AC. Underneath the initials read "Flying Ointment."

He lifted one of the glass jars out, looking for an ingredients label. Nothing.

Who the hell would send a shop unsolicited flying ointment? And not list the active ingredients? Joshua grimaced, picked up the box, and headed toward the back door that led to the large shop garbage bin.

A prickling at the back of his neck stopped him. And wasn't that interesting? He hadn't felt a thing when he tested the box, but *now* something wasn't going to let him throw the thing away?

Well, damn.

Joshua opened the purple-painted door that led to the small storeroom and set the box on one of the shelves. Then he locked the door, went back to the counter, and picked up his cell phone.

The front door jingled. It was Quanice, coming in for his shift. Right on time. The young Black man was a budding chaos magician and a solid worker. Black T-shirt. Black summer-weight cargo pants. Black low-top Converse All Stars.

Big silver chaos star on a black leather thong around his neck.

"Good morning, Quanice, welcome to The Road Home!"

"Good morning, revered employer." He stalked forward, straightening objects on shelves as he went, with his one free hand. A ragged black army bag was slung across his chest, bulging with something, and he held a go cup of coffee in the other hand.

"I brought bagels," Quanice said, setting his coffee on the counter and dragging a paper sack from his bag.

"You know my weakness. Reimburse yourself from petty cash."

As he said it, Joshua winced a little inside. The shop was not doing great lately. He hoped Faerie Fest would give them a much-needed boost of cash. But the day he couldn't afford a bagel was the day the shop closed down.

"I need to make a few phone calls. You good to start?"

"Yep. Just let me dump my bag. I'm on it."

Joshua took a warm bagel, then headed to the stock room, phone in his other hand. This needed to be a private conversation. He really hoped Brenda was already at the Inner Eye, because he was out of his depth with whatever was in that box.

7

SELENE

Brenda had tried to convince Selene to go home, but if Selene went home, they'd go to bed, and they had work to do. No work, no money. No money, no rent for the attic aerie they called home.

So Selene took their tablet to work on designs in Raquel's café. Coven members owning businesses that Selene wanted to patronize was very convenient. Maybe someday they'd make enough money to need Alejandro's IT services or have a home that required Lucy's painting expertise.

For now though, the Inner Eye and Raquel's café did just fine to round out Selene's life. Now that they'd graduated, Selene knew the coven—her friend Cassiel especially—worried that Selene would become a hermit. According to the coven, going to Goth clubs and coven meetings didn't constitute a well-rounded social life.

What did they know? Besides, the Inner Eye and Raquel's were both well warded and protected, which for an empath was a boon. Both places felt like magic. Like welcome. Like home.

Cassiel was working, red curly hair in a towering mess on top of her head, one of Raquel's red aprons on over her jeans. Raquel was on site, also clad in jeans and a T-shirt with "Raquel's Café" curved around a coffee cup with a heart in the center. The shirt was black and the text and cup were red, just like the actual coffee mug Selene was nursing right now.

They should have been drinking more mint tea, but screw it, their stomach felt okay, and they hadn't gotten much sleep the night before. Who could, after all of that?

Selene looked at the design they were in the middle of. It was actually a new ad for Lucy's company, Paint it Bright Co. The name was a spell, of course, designed to reflect what Lucy was putting out into the world, and to draw customers into her vision. Lucy wanted a more beautiful world, she said, and everything about her company needed to reflect that.

It was Selene's job to weave that spell into the ad that was going into the local weekly newspapers and had to do double duty on Facebook and the like. Selene was going to have to convince Lucy to do two ads. There was no way to convey the magic of it all in colored pixels and have it translate into black-and-gray newsprint.

The longer Selene worked with clients, the more they figured out that design wasn't always the most important part of the job. They had to also teach their clients a smattering of design theory so they could be convinced that Selene wasn't just trying to get more money out of them, but that there were solid reasons for the design choices Selene suggested.

Selene had grown more confident in navigating client interactions just in the past six months. So maybe Raquel and Brenda were right, and there was hope that their romantic nervousness would calm down, too.

At any rate, Lucy had told Selene in no uncertain terms that she trusted them and wanted feedback, so hopefully convincing her to spend money on two separate designs wasn't going to be too hard.

Cassiel plopped down on the booth bench opposite Selene, red mug filled with latte in her pale hand.

"Take a break with me," their friend said. "You're frowning at your tablet."

"Not surprised. I barely slept and then threw up this morning."

"I know. Brenda called Raquel, worried about you."

Selene tapped their electronic pencil on the tabletop. "Just great. The coven den mothers are going to give me shit for days."

Cassiel leaned across the booth.

"C'mon, Selene. It sounds like they're right to be worried. What the hell is going on?"

They looked at their friend's green eyes and gorgeous face, wondering how to explain.

"That's the problem. I'm not sure. Last night in the studio, I felt a goose walk over my grave. You know that feeling?"

Cassiel nodded.

"And then at the club afterwards, things just felt *off*. Wrong. My friend Janice was acting drunk, but Becca said she wasn't. And then I spilled my martini all over Joshua..."

Cassie held up a hand.

"Wait a minute. You were out with *Joshua*?"

Selene shook their head, cheeks burning hot. Damn it.

"*No!* I just...he just... He was there. With that guy Legis from the OTO. You know him, right? Well...I didn't see anyone else I knew when I walked in...."

"So you sat down across from the one guy you've ever had the hots for that I know of, and threw a drink at him."

Cassiel was winding Selene up, and knew it. Selene knew it, too.

"You know that's not how it happened. And besides, why are we talking about Joshua?"

Cassie's green eyes sparkled and Selene could tell she was fighting back a grin. "I don't know. Why *are* we talking about Joshua? And why did you throw your drink at him?"

Selene huffed, and shoved their coffee cup away. "I didn't throw it. I knocked it over like a clumsy doofus. But that's not what I was trying to tell you."

Selene's phone began an insistent buzzing from their overloaded messenger bag. That was weird. No one ever actually *called*.

They fished past the books, laptop, and makeup bag, fingers finally curling around the buzzing phone.

It was Legis. That was *really* weird.

They held up a finger at Cassiel, who sat, calmly sipping her latte.

"Hey, Legis! What's up?"

Ohmygodsohmygodsohmygods.

Selene felt the blood drain from their face as he talked. The words barely made sense, they just swirled from the tiny speaker and into their ear. Selene's eyes never left Cassie's face, so they saw when it changed from amused, to serious, to actively concerned.

What is it? Cassie mouthed at Selene.

Selene just shook their head, every fine hair on their arm standing up at attention.

No you don't, Selene thought. No puking. They were

ready for the weird psychic response now, and slowed their breathing way down. Half listening to Legis, they cast their attention outward, trying to follow whatever the hell it was that kept trying to attach itself, or scan their aura, or whatever it was doing that was making their stomach want to flip.

Faint. So faint. But definitely there.

"Hold on a second, Legis. Okay?"

Selene covered the mic with one hand and leaned across the table. "Cassie, something is tracking me. Can you try to sense what it is and what it's doing?"

Cassie leaned back against the high wooden booth back and closed her eyes. To anyone looking, it would seem as if she just needed to rest a minute. Selene felt Cassiel's energy change, though, and knew she was seeking. Just because Cassie's specialty was communicating with ghosts, it didn't mean her psychic skills were useless on the living.

Phone clamped to their ear, Selene glanced over at the counter. Raquel was staring, on high alert. Selene gave a quick nod. Raquel blew out a sharp breath and turned to the next customer.

"Legis? I've got to go. Thanks so much for calling me. I'll be in touch once I find out more."

Selene thumbed the phone off and watched Cassiel do her work. They closed their own eyes for a moment, but all they could really sense was unease. Dis-ease, actually. Something was actively wrong, as they had suspected, and was working very, very bad magic.

Damn it. The coven never got a break, did they? With Summer Solstice coming up, you'd think the creepy crawlies would be hiding in their caves, not out sowing mayhem.

Cassie's eyes snapped open.

"There's something there, for sure, but it's hard to get a clear signal with everyone's thoughts and energy signatures bouncing around the café. I think I caught the scent of it, though, so it should be easier to track from a quieter place."

Cassie rolled her neck and shoulders, then shook out her hands and picked up her red mug again.

"You going to tell me what the phone call was about? And you gonna tell the coven what in Goddess's name is going on?"

"That was Legis. The woman I was worried about at the club last night..."

"Janice."

Selene nodded. "She died."

"Oh my Goddess! How?"

"Looks like an overdose. They're still doing tox screens, trying to figure out what the substance was. Apparently it's not the usual stuff, so they're having to test again."

Selene's brown eyes held steady on Cassiel's. The air between them felt thick with conflicting energies of anger, worry, fear, and whatever magic still clung to Selene's skin, tainting them.

Finally, Cassie spoke. "This is really bad, Selene. And screw Summer Solstice. We're going to have to do something about it. I've got to get back to work. Call the coven. Now."

Cassie scooted out of the booth and stood, pausing as she picked up her mug. "And Selene?"

"Yeah?" Selene's heart was pounding again, panic starting to rise.

"You don't have to do this alone. And tell that part of you that's fighting right now that we've got your back."

Selene's throat closed, and they blinked away the sudden moisture that filled their eyes.

Clearing their throat, they managed a gruff, "Thanks."

"I'm sending Raquel over. And some soup. You look like

hell, which tells me along with no sleep, you haven't eaten in the last twenty-four hours."

"Thanks, Cassie."

Selene put their head in their hands, letting the long, pressed-straight black hair fall like a curtain, temporarily shutting out the world.

A few seconds of being alone might be all they were going to get right now. Selene supposed it would have to do.

8
___

JOSHUA

His living room was lit with every candle he had.

They flickered and cast shadows everywhere, heating up the room and filling it with the scent of beeswax. Covered in a light film of sweat, he had stripped off his linen shirt and tie, and wore only a white ribbed A-shirt. After his magical working, Joshua planned to go out back and look at the full moon and cool down. Meanwhile, though, he'd better either open a window or turn the AC on.

Window. He wanted the night air for his magic, not some canned flow of cold. When he lifted the old wooden casement, a slight breeze entered the room, shifting the dark green, floor-length curtains. It brought the scent of jasmine and brugmansia with it. Two of Joshua's favorite smells.

Turning toward the coffee table he'd set up as an altar between the long green couch and the damask-covered chairs, Joshua sighed.

Every single thing in the universe seemed to be telling him to get his magical shit back together. And if he was going to answer that call, tonight was the night. The full moon before Solstice was as good a time as any to get himself back on track.

He had to face himself or risk...he didn't even know what. The failure of his business? Something else?

Facing himself was a risk. But not facing himself was turning out to be worse.

And now Janice was dead. It felt unbelievable, despite what Legis had said about overdoses being all too common in his line of work. Joshua barely knew Janice, so maybe his impression of her was wrong, but he'd never gotten the sense that she was a user. Never saw her drink more than a glass of wine or two at the clubs.

Never seen her acting the way she had the night before, either. You never really knew with people. What was going to send them over the edge?

Speaking of drugs...Brenda said she didn't know anything about the flying ointment company. She hadn't gotten a box, though they both suspected that one might be on its way. He'd dropped a jar of the stuff at the Inner Eye before he opened shop for the day. Brenda said she would pass the ointment along to her coven mate Tobias. They hoped that with his herbal expertise, Tobias might be able to tease out some of the ingredients from scent alone. It was a long shot, but right now?

They couldn't exactly call the police and say that someone had given them free samples of a product. Joshua could just see how that would go. Eyes rolling, heads shaking, muttered curses about "weirdos and freaks."

So yeah. It sounded like Tobias was the current best bet. They needed more information before going to the rest of the Portland magical community. Brenda didn't want to call on the Wyrd Sisters or the others with half-cocked theories and speculation.

Wild speculation had been the cause of too many magical battles and witch wars. The Arrow and Crescent witches wanted to avoid that at all costs. Smart.

Stop delaying.

Joshua sat down at the altar. His black-handled athamé, a pendulum, and a chalice filled with cool water formed a rough triangle between two pillar candles. In the center of the triangle of tools were the three cards from his reading the day before.

If he was going to get more information, this was the best way he currently knew how.

"Back to basics."

Joshua straightened his spine, and began the long, slow, breathing practice he'd been taught years before. Back when he first studied magic. Back when it felt like it might save him, and possibly even save the world.

Inhale. Two. Three. Four.

Hold. Two. Three. Four.

Exhale. Two. Three. Four.

Hold. Two. Three. Four.

He found himself closing off his throat on each inhalation, tensing up, and adjusted his body to counteract that. Touching the tip of his tongue to the roof of his mouth, he allowed his breathing to settle and deepen. When it came time to pause between inhalation and exhalation, he held the breath by engaging his diaphragm, instead of closing off his throat.

His body recalled the pattern; all it took was this simple reintroduction. He hoped the rest proved this easy.

Feeling more centered and present, he lightly touched the blade and chalice, invoking a sense of his own will and asking for clarity of heart. That was simple intuition on his part. His current problems stemmed from his heart, and not his mind.

The chalice seemed like a way through.

That done, he turned his attention to the cards. The Lovers. The Devil. The Moon.

"What do you have to teach me? What are you trying to say? Show me...please."

He breathed out across the cards, causing the candle flames to flicker. Shadows moved across the slick surfaces, highlighting some images, leaving others in the darkness his own shadow cast over the table.

The goat stared at him with steady eyes. The King and Queen were superseded by the robed figure, holding out hands over their heads. Blessing or control? The question seemed important.

The Moon. What struck Joshua tonight were all the hidden, barely there forms, rising up from the waters. The scarab beetle pushed the sun disk up from those primordial depths, trying to reach the earth, and then the sky. Resurrection, rising from the death of ego.

He still wasn't quite getting it, though Joshua could feel the stirring of some inchoate consciousness, deep within. Keeping his breathing steady, and his spine erect, he spoke to the cards again.

"Show me. Tell me. Please."

His fingers snaked toward the pendulum, a simple point of brass, on the end of a short, brass chain.

Looping the chain between the index and middle fingers of his right hand, Joshua held the pendulum over the Moon card. He passed his hand down the chain, making certain the line of the pendulum was plumb and still.

Then he checked. Made sure he was still as centered and still as possible.

Yes.

Exhaling, Joshua focused on the card. The pendulum rocked and swayed, back and forth, very gently, the movement barely perceptible in the midst of the flickering candlelight. The back and forth motion was his pendulum's gentle "no," which in this case—since the movement wasn't emphatic—he took to mean "move on."

Glancing at the Lovers, he followed the lead of the pendulum, which seemed to be straining toward the final card instead.

The Devil.

He breathed in again, a long, slow draft. Stilled himself inside. Stilled the pendulum with a gentle pass of his hand over the chain.

Focused on the eyes of the big goat.

The pendulum moved. Rocking. Swaying. It began a small, clockwise rotation. The circle grew larger and larger with each pass, the chain pulling into a taut line, tugging on Joshua's fingers. The arc of the rotation grew so extreme, the pendulum practically flew out parallel to the coffee table, like a spinning carnival ride, pushing scooters outward by virtue of centrifugal force.

Just across the coffee table, hovering in the space between the two damask chairs, a form shimmered, taking shape.

Joshua's breath hitched in his chest. The pendulum faltered before the chain snapped taut again.

His eyes were riveted to the space between the chairs, starting to tear up from the strain of looking.

It was a goat. A huge, white goat, with slitted, golden eyes and a mighty fish's tail. Capricorn. Unforgiving discipline, ruled by restriction. Order. It tamed the flow of Pisces and disregarded the see-sawing attempts at regulation of the Twins.

And it was there for him.

He dropped the pendulum. It clattered on the table before rolling to the floor. A gust of air rushed through the open window, and the altar candles extinguished themselves, leaving climbing coils of smoke behind. The other candles in the room wavered, then flared brighter.

Joshua was truly sweating now, fighting to control his breathing. Fighting to stay upright, to not cower beneath the altar table like a groveling worm.

The goat opened its mouth. Joshua's mind filled with a rushing, roaring sound.

The sound resolved itself, forming words.

Danger. The only sin is restriction. Protect those who do not know.

Then the fish-tailed goat was gone. Joshua collapsed against the couch, panting and sweating.

It was all he could do to breathe.

The wind died down. The curtains stilled. The candles settled back into a steady glow.

Joshua picked up the chalice from the altar, and drank until the water was gone.

9

—————

SELENE

A breeze swept up off the Willamette, smelling of river and night. The full moon hung above the span of the Hawthorne Bridge, luminous, so bright. Standing in the middle of the bridge, gazing up, Selene felt dazzled. Humbled. And, even in the middle of whatever shit storm was currently brewing, in this moment? Selene felt grateful.

Lately, life around Selene felt a bit like the seven of cups from the Tarot. Stacked chalices filling up with poisonous delusion, spilling over onto everything.

If the card held any hope at all, it was in the move to the eight, where the dark night of the soul became a harbinger of dawn.

Selene really needed a sense of light. And to get clean.

"Mother Moon, lend me vision and clarify my mind. Fill me with your light. Illuminate me. Mark my path." They paused, arms upraised, barely hearing the cars passing by. "Mother Moon, guide my coven, Arrow and Crescent, so we can open the way for those in need. Help us clear any poisons running through our magic, so we can become the beacon that you are."

The wind ruffled Selene's long hair and caressed their face. It felt like a blessing. A temporary reprieve.

The whole evening felt that way. At Cassiel's insistence, Selene had texted the rest of the coven. Half of them couldn't meet tonight, and since they already had plans to get together at Raquel's tomorrow, word had come down from Raquel and Brenda that they should just wait.

So here Selene was, on the night of the full moon before the Summer Solstice, heading to a pop-up art event under the Hawthorne Bridge. Another tricky situation for an empath to navigate, Selene had begged off, but their friend Tabitha kept at them until finally, Selene relented.

So here they were, headed to a place they both would and would not belong, as usual.

They didn't let that thought enter too deeply; instead, Selene blew a kiss skyward, then turned and walked toward Tom McCall park, the small strip of grass and walkways that skirted the river between the Hawthorne and Morrison Bridges.

Their boots sturdy and satisfying beneath them, Selene walked, a long, open-front snow-white tunic belling around the long, slim black skirt they'd donned before heading out. They'd taken extra care with their makeup and jewelry tonight, as well, and felt about as good as circumstances would allow.

Sometimes the glamor of clothing and makeup changed a person enough that they could forget just how bad things were.

Selene was banking on that. It would be great if they could enjoy the art show organized by a crew of friends from school.

Tabitha was the main instigator and had asked if Selene wanted to take part, but Selene was sick of their thesis art, and hadn't finished anything that felt satisfying yet. The occult still life was only three quarters finished. Not ready to show.

The bridge rounded toward the right, forming an offramp that led to downtown. Just at the head of the offramp, stairs beckoned Selene down. They could see the lights of the park as well as colored shadows beaming up toward the concrete overpass.

The art show must be just below, exactly as Tabitha said it would be. They braced themselves, making sure they were centered and grounded and shoring up their aura with a breath.

The wall of sound hit Selene as they stomped and jingled down the stairwell. Some pop music they barely recognized, high and bright and loud. Too loud. Connected to center, they took another breath, and got ready for the onslaught of people and noise.

So much for the pop-up gallery being stealthy. Selene grinned. Tabitha never was one for hiding in the shadows.

"Selene!"

Speaking of...Tabitha bounded toward Selene, wearing a ridiculously bright yellow dress over red cowboy boots. A lesbian femme, her blond hair was up in some elaborate 'do and her lips were painted orange.

Goddess bless Tabitha. She would never go out of style because her style was all her own.

Tabitha crushed her arms around Selene's waist, her head barely reaching Selene's shoulder. Tabitha was one of the few people outside the coven from whom Selene toler-ated casual physical affection. Mostly because Tabitha was so damn *nice,* but also because she pretty much insisted upon it, in the nicest possible way.

She gave Selene a tight squeeze before releasing them again.

"You'll never guess what someone brought!" The words practically burst from Tabitha's orange lips.

"What?"

Tabitha leaned back in, as if they were conspirators. In a loud, whiskey-scented stage whisper, she said, "Flying ointment! You're a witch! I bet you know all about that, right?"

Tabitha tugged at Selene, drawing them deeper beneath the overpass, toward the colored lights, the kinetic sculptures that floated like metal buzzards overhead, and the paintings temporarily hung on concrete walls.

And the people. The crushing buzz of people.

Selene willed themself to breathe. To relax. To lighten up.

"Isn't it great? Flying ointment on the full moon! Do you want to try some?"

Selene tried to disentangle from Tabitha's grip, but once the woman took hold, it was hard to get her to let go.

"Um...not really. Thanks, though."

The lights painted Tabitha's face with blue, then red, then gold as she dragged them further in.

"Tabitha." Selene tugged her to a stop.

"What?" Tabitha's bright mouth turned down at the corners, just a bit. "What's the matter?"

"I don't think you should use flying ointment. Not that came from a 'someone.'"

"Oh, come on! What kind of a witch *are* you? Besides, I already smeared some at the base of my throat a while ago! That's one of the places they suggested. Right?"

Selene just shook their head, feeling horrified, but not knowing what to say.

"Well, all right then," Tabitha remarked. "Get yourself a

drink if you want one. Mark set up a bar under the second arch. *I* am going to fly!"

Tabitha looked hectic all of a sudden, with spots of red on her cheeks that hadn't been there before. Her smile was too bright.

"Are you okay?" Selene said, risking a hand on Tabitha's arm.

"Selene! I'm fine! I'll be fine!" And with a whirl of yellow, Tabitha was moving through the crowd.

"Just great." Selene shouldn't have come. They didn't know enough people here, and the ones they did know weren't close at all. Just people they'd had classes with. It was hard enough for Selene to bond with anyone, but when everyone worked full-time jobs on top of school, it became easier and easier to say no to the gatherings that did happen.

Selene usually begged off by saying they had a project due to a client. Sometimes it was even true.

They looked around, the bewildered feeling they often got around crowds beginning to swirl around their head. Illusion. Delusion.

Fear. Throat closing, heart racing fear. Other people's emotions.

"No," they said out loud, and strengthened their aura yet again, this time imagining pale gray energy cycling around the outer edge. Down in front, up in back. That helped. The outside thoughts and emotions slid off the energy, giving Selene more personal space. Room to breathe.

"No what?" came a voice to their right. Fuck. Caught out.

"Nothing," they said, turning toward the contralto voice. It belonged to a woman Selene knew slightly. Shaved head. Maroon Doc Martens. Jeans with holes in them and a white men's button-down shirt. A sculptor. Worked in metal, if

Selene recalled correctly. Selene gestured up toward the concrete sweep above their heads.

"Those yours?"

The woman smiled. What was her name? Jane.

"Yes, they are. Do you like them?"

Goddess, where did this woman get her confidence from? Selene would practically kill for a quarter of it. You *never* asked someone if they liked your work.

Unless you were Jane and knew for a fact that your work kicked ass and thought that anyone who didn't like it was dim.

A scream cut through the music before Selene could answer.

"Shit!" Jane said. "What's that?"

They both ran toward the spot the commotion was happening. People were milling around, some with arms raised, some with phones stuck to their ears. As they got closer, they could see a small space had been cleared and the people were clustered around it. Above the space was one of Jane's vultures, one massive wing dipping downward, as if to point at the person on the ground.

The person in the yellow dress, convulsing on the concrete floor.

"Shit," Selene said. "Get her on her side!"

As two people moved to comply, Selene rushed forward. Someone balled up a light sweater and shoved it under Tabitha's head. The skin on her face was red all over now, and her body shook and shuddered. Selene placed two fingers on her throat.

"Pulse is racing and feels jumpy. Erratic."

"Excuse me! Let me through!"

As stocky man shoved his way into the circle. Another

person Selene vaguely recognized from school. "I'm a trained EMT."

Once he saw what they'd done, though, he stopped. "Okay everyone, an ambulance is on its way. Just step back, okay?"

Someone turned off the music. Over the babble of voices, Selene heard a siren heading their way. Thank Goddess it sounded close.

"Mother, protect Tabitha. And please, protect us all."

Holy Mother. How were things actually getting worse?

10

JOSHUA

It was Solstice, a bright, summery day with temperatures threatening to hit the low 90s.

Too hot for Joshua, who far preferred the Portland rain. He shuffled some paperwork into a drawer and tapped his fingers on the counter.

It was also one of those days where, if Joshua could have stayed home, he would have. But Quanice had called in sick with a bad summer cold, and the heat seemed to be bringing people out to shop. He really couldn't complain about that last one. On sunny weekends, sometimes the shop was slow, what with people having picnics and barbecue, unless it was too hot even for that, then The Road Home got people before or after showings at the old, air conditioned, Moorish-style theater.

Today must have been one of those movie Sundays because the crowds came in waves. He'd already had to politely ask two people to not bring ice cream into the store.

Thank the Gods *his* air conditioning worked. Last year it was on the fritz and he'd had to bring in swamp coolers and fans.

At least the shoppers meant he couldn't focus too long on the weird appearance last night. The Capricorn goat-fish or fish-goat, bringing a message of danger. The entity had also spoken a phrase Joshua recognized, and he was just waiting to have a conversation with Legis about it. *The only sin is restriction* was a phrase he knew from his readings on Crowley. Thing was, in this context, he had no idea what it meant.

Oh, it had something to do with the Devil card, that was for sure. Something about not bottling up too much life force. But if the message was for him, Joshua was damned if he knew what it meant. He was being asked to look at himself, at his patterns, and to get serious about magic again. Well, part of that seemed like tapering off from dating every random babe he came across.

And wasn't discipline about curbing life force? Or was he missing something?

But the rest of the message was clearly about the weird things happening. Like Janice's death. *Protect those who do not know.*

Joshua looked around the store, at the two teenagers browsing the Magic 101 section, the way he and Jessie used to. Or the tired-looking man hovering over the ring display, as if something in there would fulfill some void inside.

When he'd asked the man if he wanted to see anything, the look of longing in his eyes shot through Joshua like a dart.

The man had mumbled a "No thanks, just looking," before wandering to the gemstones and crystals for awhile. But now he was back at the rings.

The door chimed, signaling more customers. Joshua glanced up at the mirror over the counter where he strung less expensive pendants and amulets from satin cords. An older woman with streaked champagne-blond hair. It looked as though she'd been crying.

Oh boy.

She headed straight for the shelves with the house-blended oils, as if she knew right what she was looking for. Yeah. Joshua recognized her. She liked his Rose Queen offering oil and had also bought Choose Love, which was one of Joshua's favorite blends.

She opened a few of the testers, sniffing each in turn, occasionally pausing to sniff the little canister of coffee beans he kept on the shelf next to the oils. Just like some foods were palate cleansers, sniffing coffee beans cleared the nasal passages.

Joshua went back to stringing seven-pointed stars onto teal satin cords.

"I'd like to buy this." It was the woman, holding out a vial of oil.

Protect Yourself, the label read.

"Everything okay?" he asked.

The woman jerked. Startled. "Yes! I mean...no. It's my son.... You've met him before."

Joshua nodded. Her son was a cute, athletic man just about twenty years old. Gay. At least that was the hit Joshua got from him.

"I think he's gotten himself in some kind of magical trouble," the woman continued. "There's this teacher...an alchemist or something..."

Joshua waited.

The woman shook her head. "But that's his business. I can't really talk about it."

Joshua nodded. "I'm sorry. I shouldn't have pried."

He rang her up, ran her debit card, and wrapped the vial in a piece of lavender tissue paper.

"Do you need a bag?"

"No. No thanks. My purse has a little pocket. I think it'll fit."

As he handed her the small packet, static electricity sparked. They both pulled back. The woman barely held onto the oil.

Those who do not know.

Damn it.

"Look, I know I just said I shouldn't have pried, but if your son is really in trouble, I hope you let me know. We try to take care of people in the magical community."

She swallowed and nodded, tucked the tissue-wrapped vial in her purse, and left.

He really hoped she'd be all right. And that her son wasn't dabbling in something he shouldn't be. That was one of the problems with running a shop like this. Most of the time people who said they were encountering some sort of metaphysical nastiness were puffing themselves up for drama's sake.

But sometimes? The trouble was real. And she'd mentioned a teacher, which was extra worrying....

"Excuse me?"

It was the nervous man.

Joshua forced what he hoped was a reassuring smile onto his face. "Yes?"

"May I see this medal, please?"

Joshua pulled the little set of display case keys out of his pocket and approached.

"Which one?"

"That one," the man pointed. "To the left."

Joshua's heart stopped in his chest. Just for one second. Then it started up again. The man pointed to the stylized medal of St. Michael. A crossed flame and sword.

Protection again. And the same medal Brenda's girl-friend, Caroline, had chosen back when she was being stalked by her abusive ex-husband.

Hand shaking slightly, Joshua pulled the medal out and placed it into the man's outstretched hand.

"Is everything all right?" It felt as if the words had pushed themselves from between his lips.

The man looked so damn defeated, and as if the space around him was a vacuum, ready to suck him in.

"I have no idea. But this feels like it might make things better."

"That's a pretty powerful piece there, so you're probably right."

Holy shit. Or he'd be dead within twenty-four hours from whatever the hell was trying to suck him dry.

They walked back toward the tablet Joshua used as a cash register.

The man winced a bit when Joshua told him the price, but shoved his card at Joshua anyway. That wasn't good. "Do you want a cord for this? Or I have a small gift bag I can put it in."

"Are the cords expensive?"

"They're free. What color?" Joshua gestured to the cords swimming like bright snakes on the wooden countertop.

"Red."

Joshua strung the medal, sending out a prayer to Archangel Michael to please, oh please, protect this man.

Then, reluctantly, he sent the man back out into the hot, bright day.

Finally, the shop was empty. Must be movie time.

Joshua turned to the stack of mail from the day before. There was a folded and sealed flier from Faerie Fest North-west, a big fantasy show that made up a good part of The

Road Home's revenue every year. He'd already paid for booth space and secured people to work both the shop and the show for the duration.

Slitting the round sticker holding the flier together, Joshua groaned.

After a decade of magic, we regret to inform you...

"No! *Damn* it!"

The flier fluttered to the countertop, resting on the tangle of cords.

Faerie Fest was cancelled. They would be refunding his fees within the week.

But he'd already ordered extra inventory for it. A *lot* of extra inventory. Thousands of dollar's worth.

What the hell was he going to do? This was bad. Very, very bad.

"Okay. Gods and Goddesses? Capricorn fish-goat? I'm *trying* here. You said to get my shit together, and I started. You said to help the unknowing, and I asked. So *what the fuck do I need to do to turn this around?*"

His fists clenched on the counter. Joshua banged them on the hard wood. Once. Twice. Thrice.

He hit hard enough that he'd likely have bruises the next day.

The pain felt good. Righteous. It felt like something real. A fist on wood was tangible, unlike whatever specters haunted his poor customers, and whatever the hell it was that had killed Janice.

Was it despair? Or was something more sinister going on?

"Game. Fucking. On." Joshua said. "But you want me to do this? Then you're going to have to help."

He picked up the phone. First thing, he was calling his distributors to see if they could cancel the big orders.

And after that? He was calling Legis. He needed information, and he needed it now.

And Frater Louis and Legis were the only ones he could think of who would know what the fuck the fish-goat was talking about.

And after that?

He might just call Selene.

11

SELENE

Selene felt like hell again.

It was too damn hot. There had been cool summer days in Portland, Selene knew there had. But it had been so many years, it felt hard to remember. And the way heat worked in Portland meant that the coven had picked the hottest Goddess-damned time of day to meet.

Five o'clock on a Sunday afternoon. *Hah hah, get it? Sunday?* Selene groused to themself, scurrying up the walkway that led to the back of Raquel's old four-square Craftsman house.

Selene had even trotted out their long, black linen shorts and a loose white shirt with a T-shirt beneath it to soak up the sweat. They barely wore any makeup, because sweating under a full face was just disgusting. A little waterproof mascara, tinted sunscreen, and lipstick would have to do.

Luckily, coven was family. Besides, Selene had so much going on they could barely breathe, let alone put together a proper summer outfit. Tabitha was in the hospital and Selene couldn't help but feel it was at least partially their fault.

"Whoa!" Cassiel's voice greeted Selene as they stepped through the gate into Raquel's backyard. "You know it's hot when Selene isn't wearing boots!"

Selene looked down at their black Chuck Taylors and wiggled their toes.

"I'd like to see you wearing leather in this heat," they complained.

Cassiel laughed. She actually wore a sundress, which was not her usual attire, either. It was an emerald green that blended with the lush green in Raquel's garden, and set off the red curls that flowed loose down her back.

The rest of the coven was already gathered in chairs set under the big maple that shaded most of the yard. Selene held Cassie back.

"Joshua just called me."

Cassie fought a grin. "And?"

"He asked me out. To dinner."

Cassiel smacked Selene's arm. "That's great! He's totally your type!"

Selene looked at Cassie as if she'd grown two heads.

"What? He *is*. He's Goth. He's smart. He's a great dresser. And I bet he's a great kisser, too. He's got those ruby-red lips..."

"Stop it!" Selene said, smacking Cassie back. Then everything else came crashing back in. "That isn't all.... Tabitha got rushed to the hospital last night."

"What? Oh no! Don't tell me, though. The coven needs to know."

Selene struggled to walk forward, toward the people they loved best in this world. The people who knew them and loved them back. It was too much. The grief. The confusion. The fear. And this time, the feelings were all inside Selene.

Plus, there was that feeling that somehow Selene was responsible which was completely irrational. Even Selene knew that. But that didn't mean the feeling went away.

And Cassiel still hadn't figured out what was tracking Selene, either. So they didn't know if the overdoses were connected to it.

But it sure felt as if they were.

Brenda stepped forward, dark hair up today, a long white tunic floating around her slim frame. She folded Selene into a hug. Raquel followed soon after, red loose trousers skirting her lush hips. She hugged Selene, too. Selene inhaled the goodness of these women who had given them so much. As soon as they let Selene go, it felt as if a cloud moved in front of the sun.

The other coven members rose as if to offer hugs, but Selene held up their hands, warding them off. Too much attention at once.

"Hi everybody," Selene said. "Happy Solstice. Life sucks."

"Well, life *doesn't* suck," Raquel replied. "But that makes me think we need to do our Solstice ritual before getting down to discussion. I don't know about the rest of you, but a little celebration of the light seems in order."

Selene's shoulders slumped. They should have known that, no matter what was going on, Arrow and Crescent would celebrate the fire feast together.

"Come on," Brenda said, putting one arm around Selene's back. "We didn't plan anything long or elaborate. Just a quick meditation. It'll be fine."

Selene let themself be steered to a folding chair between Tobias and Moss. They nodded at the rest of the coven members. Alejandro. Lucy. Tempest.

Raquel continued speaking. "As you know, things got a

little hectic around Beltane, what with dealing with white supremacists, and all."

There were a couple of dry chuckles at that, though they didn't have much humor in them.

"And everyone's been too busy recovering from that to want to plan. So Brenda and I decided to keep it simple. We skipped the full moon this month, it being jammed up against today, but we still wanted to do something to honor the fullness of the month and the year. Brenda?"

Brenda stood and joined Raquel. Selene could see the ways in which they truly were sisters. Two different body types, one taller and more slender, one lush and round. One with pale peach skin, one with dark brown. One a parent, the other not. One a lesbian, the other a cis hetero woman.

But the energy that moved between them rippled, almost palpable. It felt to Selene the way a windy day at the ocean felt, when the breeze kicked up and carried bright sprays of water high into the air.

That was the energy that fueled this coven. Air and water facing one another. Brenda and Raquel.

"We call to the sun," Brenda said.

"We call to the moon," Raquel replied.

"We call to the fullness of the year, to the power of earth and sky," they said together.

"Feel life, thrumming all around you," Raquel's voice took prominence. "Breathe it in. Bless it and be blessed."

Selene closed their eyes. They allowed themself to relax and sink into the cadence of Raquel's voice. Selene felt themself opening to the words, to the heat, to the scent of flowers, the calling of finch and crow, to the distant music from another backyard gathering, a few blocks away. To the way the chair dug into their thigh, and the maple towered overhead.

Life. Selene breathed it in, feeling the sticky heat of it. *Okay. You can do this, Selene.*

Brenda's voice took up the thread. "We call upon the brightness of the day. We call upon the sun at its zenith! Fill us with your light and power. Feed us well, so we may feed each other."

"Give us life!" Raquel said, voice raised to the sky.

"Give us life!" the coven shouted in reply.

The small hairs all over Selene's body rose and crackled. It wasn't just the energy the coven raised around them. It was as though something—or someone—tugged at the edges of their aura. Again. Trying to break in. Trying to take them away from themselves, away from all that felt solid and real.

Selene tugged back, resisting. The pull was strong, threatening to drag them out and under, like a sneaker wave tugging them out to sea.

A drumbeat started. Was it real? Selene didn't want to open their eyes to see.

"We are one with the brightness of the sun! We are the champions of life and day! Rising from the depths of fertile darkness, blessed by the rains of winter, blessed by the sweet light of the moon. We rise into life!" Was that Raquel speaking? Brenda? Someone else?

Selene couldn't tell anymore.

The drum grew louder. Too loud.

"We rise with the power of life! We rise with the power of life!"

Selene felt Tobias and Moss stand. Heard the coven dancing around her. Dancing to the beating of the drum.

Frozen in place, stuck in their chair, long hair sticking to their cheeks, Selene began to weep. They weren't even certain the tears were theirs. But who else's would they be?

Tabitha? Selene asked in their mind. There was no answer. The coven danced and chanted around garden, voices raised toward the sun in its full power.

"Opening to *life*! Opening to *light*! Opening to *life*! Opening to *light*!" The chanting and drumming went on and on.

All Selene wanted was the comfort of darkness, the pale light of the moon. And for whatever was attached to them to go away.

They tried to feel the grass beneath their Chuck Taylors. They tried to breathe, but the heat made that difficult. They tried to remember their magic.

They tried to remember that they were a witch. And a strong witch. A witch that had gone into battle more than once, and won at least temporary victories.

"My name is Selene," they began to whisper. "I hold the power of the moon."

Their own whispered voice was a comfort in the midst of the coven, dancing for the sun. But Selene only half believed themself.

Nonetheless, eyes still screwed tightly shut, they pushed up from their chair. Raised their arms under the shaded canopy of the maple tree. Selene cast their awareness outward, past whatever interference was messing with their auric field. Past the hum and shiver of the summer day. Searching. Searching.

Seeking out the moon. And there she was. Just past full.

Selene breathed clear again. Their skin cooled by a few degrees. A slight breeze kicked up, rustling leaves and hair and grasses.

The drumming stopped.

They heard the coven panting softly around them. A chuckle. A gasp.

"We say Hail to the sun!" Raquel shouted.

"Hail!" the coven shouted in reply.

"We say Hail to life!" Brenda shouted.

"Hail!"

"And we give thanks," Selene murmured.

"We give thanks," Moss murmured back, giving Selene's arm a gentle squeeze. A sign of connection, then gone.

Selene opened their eyes and looked around to see the coven smiling at one another. Smiling at Selene. Eyes filled with love.

"I really need your help," Selene said.

"Well then," Raquel said, "we're going to get some lemonade and the lemon poppy scones Tempest baked, then we're going to have a meeting, and see what we can do."

12

───────

JOSHUA

The temple was an unassuming storefront on a busy southeast Portland street in the midst of a rapid transition from a light industrial working-class neighborhood into something it hadn't quite decided on.

If Joshua hadn't known what he was looking at, he likely wouldn't have thought much of the burgundy curtains behind the large windows that should have been displaying the nice interior of some shop. Instead, in front of the curtains hung a burgundy banner, with the white outline of a vesica piscis. The center of a cosmic Venn diagram. Emblazoned in the center of the shape, surrounded by white rays of light, was a triangle with an eye in the center, a white dove flying downward beneath it, and a flaming chalice anchoring it all.

White letters above and below the symbols read, "Light Eternal Lodge, Ordo Templi Orientis." The Thelemic Temple, they often called themselves, *thelema* being an ancient Greek word that represented the marriage of love and a person's will. A rejection of staid Victorian Christian morality, the contemporary OTO had more members than had ever joined in its supposed heyday, when the white, middle-class artists, poets, and actors had formed two magical lodges: The Hermetic Order of the Golden Dawn, and slightly later, the OTO.

And not long after, Gerald Gardner and Doreen Valiente had founded what would become modern Wicca. They took the older forms of witchcraft, pagan worship, herbalism and the like, and blended them with some of the ceremonialist rites, making a witchcraft for a new age.

Joshua mused on this, sweating on the busy street, waiting for someone to answer the bell. He found the history interesting and wondered if knowing too much about how the sausage had been made influenced his lack of willingness to join with any single group so far.

The fact that he now questioned his former decision didn't mean he was going to join anything wholeheartedly, though. Despite being a believer, Joshua remained skeptical that there was any one true path for him.

He had never realized before how that made him feel a little lonely.

The door opened onto a diminutive Latinx man with salt-and-pepper hair. Dressed all in black, Frater Louis had made two concessions to the heat. His black shirt was a loose, short sleeved guayabera, its neat pin-tuck pleats running down the front of the shirt on either side of the buttons. And on his feet were black leather sandals.

Joshua, wearing black linen trousers and a white linen shirt, had to admire a man who didn't wear shorts no matter the season.

"Frater Louis! Thank you so much for meeting with me."

"Blessings of the invincible sun! What say we get you into some shade."

Behind the glass and curtains, the space felt blessedly

cool. The walls were lined with bookcases. A large round study table sat off to the side. Between a pocket kitchen and a door that read WC in black letters were two stacks of chairs.

Joshua knew the actual temple was behind a set of double doors. This was just their study room, as well as a meeting and classroom space.

His tall, redhaired brute of a friend rose from behind the table.

"Legis! Hey brother, good to see you."

The two men hugged as Frater Louis got cold sparkling water from the mini fridge and ferried it to the table along with glasses filled with ice.

Joshua could have kissed the man. He mopped at his face with a rapidly wilting handkerchief and sat down, accepting the water with a smile of gratitude.

"So, Legis tells me you had a vision while working with the Thoth Tarot?"

Joshua set down the water, but kept his right hand gripped around it, still trying to get cool.

"Yes. I pulled out some cards I was working with to try and get more information last night. During the full moon. The three cards were the Lovers, the Devil, and the Moon. They all seem to have something to do with me, of course, but I kept getting the sense that they were pointing to some larger issue, too."

Frater Louis nodded, taking small sips from his glass.

"Just tell him, Joshua," Legis said. "I already gave him some of the context. He needs to hear the vision."

Joshua crossed and uncrossed his legs, then inhaled.

"Okay. A goat appeared. I swear it was in the room. It formed itself right between my living room chairs. But it wasn't the Devil goat itself. It was Capricorn."

"The goat with the tail of a giant fish," Frater Louis said. "Cardinal Earth. It's interesting to me that the three cards were mutable water, mutable air, and cardinal earth. But please, go on."

Louis gestured, and Joshua's eyes darted back and forth in their sockets, searching his brain for the thread.

"It wasn't lost on me that the cardinal force was the one to make an appearance," Joshua said. "But anyway, the fish-goat appeared. Stared right at me. It had a message. 'Danger. The only sin is restriction. Protect those who do not know.'"

Joshua paused for another drink of water. "It freaked me out a little, to be honest. And while I can probably figure out the 'danger and protection' parts of the message, that central Crowley quote baffles me."

Frater Louis smiled, then looked up at an angle, toward the bookcases on the wall behind Joshua. He cleared his throat and began a recitation.

"Sin is defined as Restriction: that is; the setting of limits, or the desire to set limits, to any thing that is, seeing that as above set forth the true Nature of all things is to fulfill themselves in all Ways. Yet though all things be thus lawful in themselves, it is often Restriction to act, and Freedom to refrain. For that Freedom is worth the other, and each case must be judged by its own Nature."

Joshua recognized the quote, though there was no way he could have recited even one sentence of it from memory like that.

"So what does it mean?" Joshua asked. "Part of my confusion is what it means for *me*. I keep getting messages that I need to step up my magical game again. I've let things slide. But that requires discipline. Will. I don't get how that doesn't mean restriction."

Legis spoke. "'It is often Restriction to act, and Freedom

to refrain.' That's the key right there. When the magician knows her will, she knows when action or refraining from action are called for."

"And that's different from restriction, how?" Joshua was starting to sweat again, despite the cool water and the air flowing through the floor vents nearby.

Frater Louis leaned toward him. "When a magician knows her will, everything she does is in the flow. Let's call on a different system. The Tao. Wu wei. You're familiar?"

Joshua mopped his brow again. "Yes, of course. Non-action. Not planning. Going with the flow."

"That's only the top layer of the concept. Going with the flow in this case doesn't mean bumping along with whatever happens to you in life. It means getting so clear inside yourself you tap the greater flow, and therefore, action or inaction, you aren't pushing the wheel. You are one with the wheel." Frater Louis paused, tilted his head and smiled. "You see?"

Joshua's brain raced to make the connections Frater Louis was trying to map out. He could just barely feel them, as if the concepts were just outside his field of vision, or comprehension.

He shook his head.

"Most people fight their lives, instead of living them. Or they get crushed by them," Legis said. "I think that's your connection between the 'protect the unknowing' message and 'the only sin is restriction' message."

Legis leveled his gaze at Joshua, eyes intent. Joshua felt everything inside himself snap to attention, waiting for the words.

"Capricorn came to give you not only a warning, but a smackdown. You've been acting like a person with no knowledge, when as a matter of fact, you are a fucking magician." Legis smacked his hand on the table. The sweating glasses jumped on their coasters.

"Man up, Joshua. Stop messing around. Harness your will. If a being as powerful as this showed up for you? It's a pretty big sign. I'm frankly more than a little worried about that larger danger message, and we're sure as hell going to need to discuss that, but the message for you? It's clear as day."

Joshua bristled at the "man up," hating that term. But he took Legis's point. He had to. But...

"So what do I need to do?" he said, trying not to sound like a mewling jerk.

"You need to look at the ways you've been living your life," Frater Louis said, calm and cool as a cucumber, despite the thick emotions in the room. "You need to take a clear, hard look at what restricts you. Keeps you in chains. Diminishes your life force and your power. And why."

His gaze caught Joshua's with so much kindness, Joshua could have wept.

"Some people are truly chained by their circumstances. Grinding poverty. Abuse so hideous we don't even want to imagine it. Any number of things that humans create to control one another rather than letting each person live his will, as he wills. But you, Joshua? That isn't you. You've only chained yourself."

Tears filled Joshua's eyes then, but he held Frater Louis's gaze, unflinching, the truth of the man's words penetrating every cell in his body.

"That isn't true," Joshua said. "My partner was taken away from me."

"And you're finally ready to deal with it," Louis replied calmly. "That's good. We can help you."

They sat that way for a while, three men around a table, breathing together.

Finally, Joshua wiped his face.

"So what do I do?" he repeated.

"You have a lot of options, brother," Legis said. "Just choose one. Stick with it for a while. Train yourself again. Train with us if you want to."

Legis stretched his big hands across the table, and pried Joshua's hand from the glass. Then he held Joshua's hands in his own.

"Get free. Then figure out how to help other people get free, too."

Joshua, never a crier, couldn't stop the tears.

13

SELENE

They were still in Raquel's garden, and it was still hot, though the cold lemonade was helping. Selene felt calmer, though a little wrung out. Alejandro had added a splash of rum to Selene's glass, and Selene had to admit, that was helping too.

The witches of Arrow and Crescent used alcohol pretty deliberately. It was one of the things Selene appreciated about them. Oh, they weren't immune to the charms of a good party, but they also knew how and when to use alcohol medicinally. On occasion, a small amount of booze could help modulate wide open psychic channels, easing the openings to smaller, more manageable wavelengths.

The untrained psychic often misused alcohol, it being the only tool they had to slam things shut when things got frightening or overwhelming. Arrow and Crescent made damn certain every member had the tools to bring themselves and one another back into alignment when the magical workings grew more powerful than most humans could stand. They had the tools to navigate the astral planes properly, and were trained to meet the Powers, the Elements, the Goddesses and Gods.

And some days? They helped you out with a splash of rum in ice cold lavender lemonade when you'd had too many days of intensity in a row.

They'd been discussing the overdoses and the case of flying ointment that had shown up on the stoop of The Road Home. Most of the coven agreed that the two things felt too synchronous to not be connected, especially given that Tabitha had offered Selene some ointment, and then ended up in the hospital pretty shortly after.

Word was that the seizures were preceded by heart arrhythmia. Something was short-circuiting people, and doing so pretty quickly, if Tabitha was an example.

"We never catch a break these days, do we?" Alejandro said. "There's no breathing room to just do our jobs and enjoy being a coven anymore."

"We are here to serve," Brenda reminded him.

"Yes, of course we are." Alejandro gestured with his lemonade. "But that doesn't mean I don't want to just enjoy a holiday for once this year."

Selene had to agree but felt too wiped out to even nod. They took another drink of spiked lemonade.

"I hate to be even more of a Solstice party-pooper," Moss said, rummaging through his messenger bag, black faux hawk bobbing as he attempted to peer inside. The cavernous purse Moss called his Bag of Holding was so loaded with pins, patches, and buttons, Selene could barely tell it started out khaki. *Not Your Asian Sidekick* read one button. *Black Lives Matter* said another. There was also a Hufflepuff school crest patch, which was pretty damn endearing. Just like Moss. One of the newer coven members,

Moss didn't always say much, deferring to Brenda and Raquel unless he had something solid to contribute.

Moss pulled a crumpled flier from his bag and smoothed it out over his thigh. "I pulled this off a corkboard at Daily Grind," he grinned. "Sorry Raquel, but I date other coffee shops."

Raquel gave a *pfft* and a wave.

"Any of you heard of this guy?"

He held up the flier. *The Shamanic Mysteries* it read, in bold, black letters.

"Hoo, boy," Raquel said. "You better read us the rest of that."

Moss cleared his throat. "Have you ever wondered if there was more to life than meets the eye? Have you ever wanted to tap into the power of your mind? Have you ever longed to journey to realms unseen? You are not alone."

"Damn it," Alejandro groused. "Who the hell are these people?"

That made Selene smirk a little. Totally upstanding, and a little tight-laced, Alejandro hated anything that smacked of a charlatan taking advantage of noobs.

"But wait," Moss held up a finger, "there's more! 'Uncover the secrets known by alchemists and shamans of old. Unleash the power of magic and change your life.'"

Moss passed the flier to Raquel, who was holding out her hand, lips tight and brow furrowed. She was working on a mad, which, if Selene weren't so wiped, and the situations they were dealing with weren't so serious, might have been amusing.

"Who the hell blends alchemy, shamanism, and who knows what other forms of magic and tries to sell it to people?" Raquel said.

"Fools," Brenda replied. "Can I see that? The flying oint-ment jars Joshua brought in mentioned alchemy."

Brenda hovered one hand over the flier, trying to sense an energy signature. After a few moments, she shook her head, silver drop earrings shaking.

"Nope. My psychometry's just not good enough. Lucy? If I get you a jar of that ointment, can you see if there's a connection? Joshua gave one to me and I left in my car."

Every witch in the coven had their specialty. While most people were fluent in several magical and psychic tech-niques, it was great to be able to draw on someone's partic-ular strength when needed. The array of skillsets made the coven a stronger, more cohesive whole.

While Brenda went off to her car, Lucy closed her eyes and attempted to tune in to the flier.

The housepainter's blue sundress floated around the chair she was sitting on, caught by a welcome breeze. Selene watched, always interested in how other people's skills worked. Selene thought of the design that still needed finishing, trying to capture a bit of Lucy's essence in their mind as she worked. Perhaps Selene could weave a bit of Lucy's magic into the ad. Something to entice customers. To set Lucy's business apart.

Brenda scurried back into the yard. "I'm sorry. It got melted in the car, so be careful with it."

Lucy opened her eyes and held out a hand, keeping the flier anchored with the other. Her pale brown hand closed around the two-ounce glass jar. Selene felt as Lucy's breath deepened and slowed down. They could almost sense Lucy's ætheric body simultaneously opening to the paper and the jar.

"I need the table," Lucy said, eyes opening again. Alejandro set up a chair at the white wrought iron table as

Moss and Raquel cleared the lemonade, scones, and rum to one side. Clutching the jar and paper, Lucy sat down.

"Thanks." Then she started the whole process again. After three minutes listening to the distant party, a chattering squirrel, and the clink of ice cubes in lemonade glasses, Lucy shook her head.

"There's something there, but I can't get a clear enough read on either the jar or the flier." She looked at Brenda and then over to Raquel. "I want to open the jar."

"I really wouldn't do that," Brenda said. "We don't know what's in there."

Lucy looked at Raquel again. Raquel shrugged. "I think Brenda's right. But I'm also not going to stop you."

Lucy cracked open the lid of the jar. Brought the half liquid ointment close to her face and sniffed. Her mouth turned down slightly. "Tobias?" she asked. "What do you smell?"

Tobias set down his lemonade and got up from his chair. When he got to the table, hands behind his back so as not to touch anything, he sniffed.

"Well...along with the base oils, I smell traces of the usual. Some datura. Belladonna. Mugwort. A little cannabis... Salvia." He sniffed again, then stood, rubbing a hand over his soul patch, dark hair flopping over his pale forehead. "There's something else I can't identify though."

Lucy stuck a finger in the jar.

"Lucy!" Brenda said. "What in Goddess's name do you think you're doing?"

Lucy closed her eyes again and rubbed the fingers of her right hand together, clearly trying to get a sense of the salve. "I can't get a proper hit on this and it's driving me crazy. I can almost *taste* the person who made this and..."

Selene saw sweat pop up on Lucy's face. Was it there before? Just from the temperature.

"Oh no," Lucy moaned.

Raquel was instantly at her side. "What's happening?"

Lucy smacked her left hand against her temple. "Headache. Bad. Nausea."

"Tobias?" Raquel asked, eyes never leaving Lucy.

"None of those herbs should have that effect. I mean, they could, but only in concentration. And not that quickly."

"Shit," Selene said, leaping up. It all came rushing in. Janice. Tabitha. "She's being poisoned! Tobias! What do we need to do?"

Lucy's pupils dilated.

Tobias grabbed Lucy's right hand and plunged it into the pitcher of lemonade. Raquel picked up a napkin, grabbed the lid, and quickly screwed it back on the jar.

"Stupid, stupid, stupid," Raquel said. "Moss! Go in the kitchen and get a bowl, dish soap, and a towel!"

Moss ran off toward the house. Raquel ran to the garden hose, cranked the valve open, and ran back to the table. "Get her hand out of the lemonade!"

Tobias yanked Lucy's hand out, and held it away from the table. Raquel squeezed the hose trigger and doused Lucy's fingers with hard spray. Selene felt the spray hit their legs.

"Tobias! Get her hand closer to the ground. I don't want this stuff flying off her skin and hitting someone."

Tobias got Lucy down to the ground, holding her as Raquel drenched them both.

Moss ran back with a bowl, towel and soap.

"Forget the bowl! Just dump the soap on her hands! But don't touch her fingers!"

Moss squirted pale yellow, viscous liquid over Lucy's

hands. Lucy rubbed her hands together as the soap and water cascaded to the grass. Moss squirted more soap. Lucy scrubbed and scrubbed her hands.

Selene watched, aghast, helpless to do anything else. They felt that creeping, lifting sensation along their skin again. And then a slight tug. *No!* Selene practically shouted the word, imagining their ætheric body flaring, shoving whatever it was away.

Alejandro stood next to Selene and pulled them close. Selene wrapped an arm around his trim waist, trying to hold themself together.

"You okay?" he murmured near their ear. Selene just nodded. They looked up at his profile, and the sheen from the hose on his face. Should Selene tell him about whatever it was? The hook or whatever it was that Cassiel sensed in their aura, and that they never got around to talking about today?

It barely seemed important anymore.

"Okay. Okay. Stop," Tobias said. "If there are still toxins on her skin, we can't reach them. Lucy, we've got to get you to urgent care now, okay?"

Raquel released the hose trigger. The summer sounds returned. Finches. A hummingbird in dive. Music.

Moss handed Lucy the dishtowel. She began to dry her hands, then moved to wipe her wet legs.

"Lucy," Moss said, "Don't touch the rest of you with that towel, okay? I'll run and get a bath towel from the house."

"Let's get you up," Tobias said, arms around Lucy, helping her to stand.

"I'll get my car," Raquel said.

14

JOSHUA

Legis, kindly, would not let Joshua go home, so the men were at a pizza place in NE Portland, not too far from Joshua's house. Every window was wide open. The outdoor patio was packed. But Legis knew the couple that owned HearthFire and had been able to score one of the few two tops in the place. Every other slab of wood was occupied by parties of four to eight, all in varied phases of party mode.

With a pitcher of local lager in between them, and a large pie on the way, Legis seemed intent on getting Joshua to reveal all of his secrets. Trouble was, Joshua had spent years avoiding those selfsame secrets, so articulating them was proving difficult. Even after his waterworks at Light Eternal Lodge.

The lager was crisp and cool, which was good, because the restaurant was overly warm.

"I don't know how the guys working the ovens stand this," he remarked.

"I wouldn't want the job," Legis replied. "Give me drug addicts over sweating in front of a massive open flame, any day. Even midwinter, it's got to suck."

They both drank.

It was clear Legis was just waiting him out now.

"I feel so stupid," Joshua finally said.

"And why is that?"

Joshua swallowed. Drank some beer. Looked out the window at a young Black couple feeding pizza to three small kids. They looked like they were having a blast, which was nice. Too often, Joshua saw parents of young kids and they just looked tired. The dad wiped a smear of sauce from the youngest boy's face. The boy high-fived his father with a tiny, chubby hand.

"I feel stupid for taking so long to figure out what's going on with me. I feel stupid for slacking. For God's sake, I own a damn esoteric shop!" He drank more beer. "I feel stupid for all the years I've run away from..."

The pizza arrived, carried by a short, skinny white woman with a shaved head and three piercings above her right eyebrow. She set the pizza stand on the table with a flourish, and placed the giant pie perfectly in the center of the wire ring.

"Get you anything else?" she asked.

"No, thank you," Legis replied. Before he even finished the sentence, she was on the move.

Legis poked one of the slices, then poured more lager into their pint glasses. He must have decided the cheese needed to cool down.

"Run away from what?" he asked.

"Myself." But no. That was only part of it. "Jessie... Love."

"Ah. The old *fear of confronting our desires* move."

"What do you mean?"

Legis grabbed a slice of pizza and transferred it to his plate. He shoved a bite of pepperoni, mozzarella, and arugula into his mouth and chewed. Then he did it again.

Joshua grabbed a slice for himself and took a bite.

"Gods, that's good."

Legis nodded and dabbed his face with a napkin.

"I really wish you were a Thelemite. It would make explaining all of this so much easier." He scratched his chin, then picked up his diminishing slice and took another bite. Joshua could practically see the wheels turning as Legis chewed.

He took two more bites of his own slice before Legis spoke again.

"People think desire is bad. It isn't. We just can't be attached to the outcome, right? That's what trips us up. People get so attached to what they think love should look like, or work, or success. So they miss what love or success actually are. Uncle Al talks about 'Pure will, unassuaged of purpose, delivered of lust of result.'"

Legis wiped his hands on his napkin and took another swig of beer.

"You didn't get the result you thought you wanted, so you gave up your will and purpose. Happens all the time."

Legis grabbed another slice.

Joshua sat back in his chair.

"Holy shit," he said. It was as if everything about the past five years had been instantly illuminated. "You're right. You're fucking right. I couldn't bring her back, no matter what I did, so I think I just started to fade away."

Joshua grabbed a second slice, but before he took a bite, he had to ask.

"So, what do you think I should do now?"

"Eat pizza. Drink beer. Enjoy these people. Enjoy the heck out of all of it."

Joshua chewed. Swallowed. Drank some more beer.

"I see what you're getting at," he said. "But it's not enough, and you know it."

Legis put down his slice again, looking slightly annoyed at the interruption of his own enjoyment.

Tough. He was the one who'd insisted on coming out in the first place. If Joshua had to suffer through himself, Legis had to, too.

Legis finally shrugged. "I don't know, man. That's up to each person. We all have to figure out will and desire for ourselves. But if I were you?"

"Yeah?"

Legis raised his pint glass, gesturing for Joshua to do the same.

"I would join Light Eternal Lodge and get serious about studying again."

Then he clinked his glass to Joshua's and made a toast.

"Ninety-three, my man. Love is the law, love under will."

"Ninety-three," Joshua replied. The standard, coded response for the Thelemic in-crowd.

Then he raised his glass again. "To love."

As Joshua drank, he felt like maybe, just maybe, things would turn around for him again.

SELENE

"It's all too much, isn't it?" Selene said. "Though at least we got the ointment off Lucy in time."

Tobias matched their slow stride as the two of them walked along the Willamette. Selene felt too keyed up to do work for their clients but knew painting would feel soothing. They would try to squeeze it in between this meeting and heading to the hospital to see Tabitha. They should probably visit Lucy, too, though Lucy was at home and was likely already grumpy from being fussed over.

Yeah. With everything going on, Selene really needed to do some art today.

It turned out that the ointment had been dosed with nicotine. The urgent care people had tested it and sent the rest of the sample to the police. Hopefully that would help the city get on top of any other random cases that showed up.

"Thank the Goddesses Lucy's okay. But I want to kill that 'alchemist' or 'shaman' or whatever they're calling themselves. Who *does* this to people?" Tobias said.

Selene stopped to look out across the water, toward

downtown. Kayakers and dragon boat teams competed for the early morning water, slicing through, barely leaving any ripples in their wake. The river smelled of silt and industry. It was cooler here than in Selene's attic, which they appreciated. They really needed to get a second swamp cooler up there. The central air to the old converted building never quite seemed to make a dent in the aerie.

"You and I both know people can be awful to other people. How many times have you been bashed?"

Tobias took in a shuddering breath, standing by their side. Selene heard him hold it, then release the air in a loud gust.

"Twice. You?"

Selene shook their head, black hair swirling around their face, lifted by the slight breeze off the river. "Too many close calls to count. But actually getting the shit beaten out of me? Three times."

"Why don't you train? I mean, look at you. You're tall. You could probably put on a little muscle."

Selene turned to their coven brother. They didn't blame him for the question. It was one they'd turned over in their own mind, many times.

"Because I don't want to," Selene said. It really was that simple. Selene didn't want to carry a gun in their purse. Didn't want to learn how to break out of choke holds or bust someone's nose with their elbow.

The only offensive action they were willing to take was with their magic. And they'd done that plenty of times. But training in physical violence? No. For some reason, that felt too much like giving in. Don't ask them why the magic was different. It just was.

The magic...came out of will and air. From the power of

nature and Selene's own talents. And a person had to be doing something very, very harmful for Selene to let it loose.

Of course, so far they hadn't used that kind of magic for themself. Only for other people. Other people's danger always felt so much worse than their own.

Selene and Tobias fell back into step, heads turned toward the water, watching a green cargo vessel chug on by. Time to change the subject.

"So. Tobacco. Did you figure that?" Selene.

Tobias grimaced. "I should have known by the symptoms you described. They were pretty classic nicotine poisoning symptoms. The dilated pupils. Headaches. Nausea. Racing heart. Trouble is, I never in a million years would think some idiot would put a concentrated dose of liquid nicotine into fucking flying ointment!"

Indignation radiated from Tobias's skin. Selene could practically feel him vibrating.

"Tell me more about it."

Tobias let out another gusty exhalation.

"Do you want to sit down awhile?" Selene asked. They approached a little seating area near the water fire station.

"No. Too keyed up. But let's walk out to the railing."

They passed through a small concrete courtyard in front of the fire and rescue station. It jutted out onto the river just enough to provide a nice view.

Leaning against the metal railing, they watched the boat traffic again, saw the cyclists across the river whirring by. Selene regretted not bringing coffee.

"So," Tobias began. "One of the reasons I'm so pissed off..."

"Besides some psychopath poisoning people?"

"Yeah. Besides that. The poisoning is heinous enough,

and this person is perverting alchemy, for one thing. But worse than that?"

He stared out over the water, jaw working as he ground his teeth. His usually beautiful face had a hard cast to it today. Selene didn't blame him.

"The dude—granted, we don't know the person's gender yet but—the dude is using *sacred tobacco* and calling what he's doing *shamanism.*"

"Insult to injury."

Tobias whipped toward Selene. "Hell yes, it's adding insult to injury! Stealing spiritual practices from the First Nations, luring people in with false promises, and then *using the plant to poison people*?"

They both turned back toward the river.

"It's unconscionable," Tobias said.

Selene tapped their rings against the hollow metal railing. Pursed their lips. "Do you get any sense that the person manipulating the plants is tied to me?"

"What do you mean?" Tobias asked.

"Well, those strange sensations I've been having, like someone's walking on my grave. The weirdness in my aura. The vomiting..." Selene's mouth twisted.

Tobias held his hands out. "May I?"

Selene nodded.

He closed his eyes and began running his hands past Selene's face, and down their arms, not touching skin. Touching only the ætheric body that surrounded their skin.

"It's hard to tell, but it does feel as if there's a connection." He opened his eyes again. "I think the flier, the ointment, and whatever's going on with you are all connected. But what I want to know is how in the world this person got hooked into you."

"Trust me, I'd like to know that, too."

Selene tapped the railing again, three times. Getting restless with all the talking.

"So, what do we do?" they said.

"I've been thinking about that. Was up half the night, trying to figure it out."

"And?"

He swallowed, hard. As if the words were hard to say.

"I'm going to use my relationship with the plants to track this fucker down. And then you?"

He turned, dark eyes boring into Selene's own. "You're going to take this asshole down."

Selene nodded. If they were built for anything, it was this sort of dark magic, it seemed. The Gods returned them to it, again and again. The bindings. The curses. The twisting of evil back upon itself.

Maybe Selene was just designed for darkness. Built for it. Standing here, on this beautiful river, on this gorgeous summer day, it sure seemed like it.

Goddess, what else do you want from me?

Nobody replied.

Maybe it was just too bright out for any answers to be revealed.

16

JOSHUA

Joshua hurried off the bus, so intent on getting to the Inner Eye right after opening that he almost barreled into a houseless man fishing for recyclables in the trash can.

"Sorry, man. Really sorry."

"That's okay," the man said in a solemn tone. "The Gods move not for those who rush, but reward those who walk carefully. I always walk carefully."

"What?" Joshua's head whipped back around, mouth open.

"Watch your step," the man replied. Then winked.

Joshua stumbled off the curb, barely catching himself and his insulated coffee mug. A car honked.

Joshua hurried across the street as fast as his new limp would allow. Safely on the opposite sidewalk, he turned back to wave at the man. The man was already pushing his cart, on his way. And damned if he wasn't walking carefully.

Okay, Gods. I get it. Messages are everywhere.

Joshua had spent half the night reading Crowley. The man brought through some real juice, tainted as it was by his rebellion against his mother and Victorian-era Christianity. Joshua felt like he wanted to study some more. To figure out whether or not he should take the plunge and get the Minerval initiation, Grade 0, which was kind of a pre-initiation rite, the first step toward actually joining a temple or lodge.

As he walked past the shops opening up for the day, ankle aching, smelling those damn delicious bagels again, he could practically feel Legis shaking his head from afar.

Legis had told him, point blank, "just choose." Not ponder. Not consider. Just choose.

But that was Joshua's problem, wasn't it? What if he chose wrong? Or what if he chose right and it was snatched away from him?

Like Jessie.

But Legis was right. Joshua knew it. He had to "frock up," as writer S. Bear Bergman would say, and just take a step. Any step.

Because he'd been taking the "no steps" for a while now, and worse than leading him nowhere, it was causing things to fall apart.

Well, his current choice was to shove open the glass door to the Inner Eye, past the clanging bells, stop inside the door, and breathe. The incense today was rosemary and California sage. The music was Loreena McKennitt.

And here came Brenda, quizzical smile on her face. Eyes creased at the corner from so many years of just that sort of smile. Moonstone shining at her collarbone.

Moonstone. That felt like a message, too, but Joshua didn't know exactly what it was.

Just keep paying attention, he thought. *Step carefully.*

Brenda's smile turned to a slight frown. She glanced down at his shoes. "Are you all right?"

Joshua followed her gaze. Damn it. Sure enough, he'd scuffed his right wingtip shoe when he stumbled off the curb. The burgundy leather was abraded. Unfixable. The wingtips would never hold a proper polish again.

"Um. I tripped. I'm okay, but...no. I'm not all right."

Brenda looked around at the empty shop.

"Let's duck into the back for a moment. I'll make us some tea."

"I don't want to take up too much of your time. I just came in to show you something."

"Come back anyway. Tempest will be here in a few minutes. She can mind the store while we talk."

Brenda paused, hand on the purple Celtic knot design curtain. "Do *you* have time?"

Joshua pulled his pocket watch out from his trouser pocket. "The store is closed Mondays so I'm good. There's always work to do, as you know, but yes, I have time."

I have nothing but time, if I listen to Legis.

"*Until you choose, your time is not your own,*" he'd said. "*Notice how you spend it. Notice what a waste most of your efforts are.*"

Cheery, supportive friend, that Legis.

So Joshua let Brenda make him tea, and helped her carry it to the little reading nook at the back of the shop. The reading nook wasn't for reading books; Brenda had comfy chairs for that. It was a curtained alcove with a small table and two chairs. When a psychic reader was with a client, they pulled the curtains shut for privacy. Today, the floor-length curtains were tied back.

As they sat down, the door chimes jangled.

It was Tempest, coming in for her shift. The back and sides of her head were freshly shorn and fresh purple dye festooned the long fall at the top, which was tied into a high ponytail today. She was holding a box.

"Hey Brenda, didn't you see this package on the doorstep?"

Brenda frowned. "There wasn't any package when I came in. Joshua?"

"I didn't see anything, either. But I was slightly distracted."

"Take it in the back and see what it is."

But Tempest kept walking toward them, sneakers silent as she crossed the floor.

"Tempest?" Brenda asked.

Tempest said nothing, just wove her way through the display cases and bookshelves, stopping in front of them, she plopped the small cardboard box on the table.

"I'll be damned," Brenda said.

The label read *Alchemical Creations* in bold, cursive script.

"The bastard," Joshua said.

"Yep," said Tempest. "So what do we do? Take it to the police? I know they're not our biggest fans, and vice versa, but…"

Arrow and Crescent had tangled with the cops a couple of times in the past year, all for good causes, but Tempest was right. The cops wouldn't exactly see it that way.

"I think we're going to have to," Joshua said. "And I should probably show them this, too."

He reached into his black leather purse and pulled out a note printed in the same damn cursive font.

How did you like the flying ointment? It read.

"That constitutes a clear threat," Brenda said.

"I thought so, too, but wanted confirmation."

The bells at the front set up clamoring again. A couple of women, chatting away.

"I'll get them," Tempest said. "Just let me throw my bag in the back."

Brenda turned her attention back to the note. "Who is this person? And why in the world are they doing all of this?"

She looked up at Joshua. "Do you know how expensive it is to make good flying ointment?"

"Well, we don't know that it's good..." Half a joke. Not funny.

Not funny at all.

"Tobias seemed to think it had all the right ingredients in it, though he'd have to test it to be sure, and there's no way for him to do that, of course. And he said it smelled like a high quality base, too. Besides all of that, I can't imagine liquid nicotine comes cheap."

"Especially not in a concentration that would cause such massive reactions."

Joshua ran both hands over his head and leaned back. He tapped his pointer finger against his lips. Trying to think. He needed to trim his goatee.

Focus, Joshua. Basics. Feet. Hands. Breath. His butt in the chair. Joshua sent his awareness to them all.

His spine straightened, rising up from his pelvis. One rotation of his shoulders, a centering of his head. He flexed his fingers. Planted both feet on the floor and stood.

Then he chose.

"I'm going to find this person, Brenda. Or I'm going to make myself so damn appealing they'll come back to find *me.* But either way? I'm going to do everything I can to bring them down."

Brenda stood, too. She touched his cheek with one cool hand.

"I see that around you, Joshua. Welcome home."

Then Tempest was moving back toward them, raising her voice just loud enough to carry.

"Boss? You need to come hear what these two women have to say."

Joshua looked up toward the front of the shop where the two white women stood, staring back at them. They weren't chattering happily anymore.

"What's happening?" Brenda asked.

"They wanted to know if we had any books on shamanism. When I asked them how they became interested, they said they had just signed up for a class."

"Shit," Joshua said.

"We'd better go talk to them," Brenda said. "Joshua? You still have time?"

"All the time in the world," he said.

17

SELENE

Selene hated hospitals. There were doctors in hospitals. And machines. And psych wards.

All of this reminded Selene too much of a childhood spent getting tests run. Getting poked and prodded. Strange people touching them. The incessant questioning. Trying to figure out if the panic attacks could be treated with drugs. Or if Selene's insistence on wearing dresses instead of a baseball uniform could be cured. Or if their shyness was just them, being stubborn.

Thing after thing after thing about Selene that other people decided must be wrong.

Becoming a teenage Goth only made everything worse.

So, it wasn't hospitals, per se, though the combined scent of bubble gum cleaning solution, rubbing alcohol, and piss and vomit with a pure oxygen chaser didn't make Selene exactly comfortable. Too many of those scents had haunted their childhood.

It all felt like one, big, never-ending punishment for just being who they were.

Selene wore their boots today, heat be damned. They'd

stopped in at the studio space after their river walk with Tobias and decided that painting was important enough that they could take an hour out for it. Then they texted Lucy, who was grumpy—just as Selene expected—but feeling okay. After cleaning up, the black canvas Chuck Taylors they'd begun the day with had been left in their studio locker, replaced by black leather Demonia buckle boots.

The boots made Selene feel confident, better able to walk through these liminal spaces where death and life chased down a conversation with each other. If Selene was going to face the horror show, they were going to do so feeling as much themselves as possible.

They'd never been allowed to do that as a child.

Selene passed the nurses' station and averted their eyes from someone crying in one of the rooms. The weird fluorescent white and medical-machine green were everywhere they turned. Selene focused on the small number plaques set to the right of every door. Steady as you go.

Tabitha should be right up ahead. There it was. 1718. She'd been moved out of ICU last night. That was the only reason Selene was able to visit in the first place. But apparently, Tabitha still wasn't doing well.

Poking first their head, then dragging their long limbs into the room, Selene covered their mouth and nose. It didn't smell any worse in here, but the enclosed space made all the concentrated *hospitalness* too much.

There was a window in the room, at least, and the curtains were open, letting the bright, midday sun stream in. It washed the room in pale yellow, softening the harshness of the white and glowing green.

Breathing into their hand for a moment, Selene fought to slow their breathing down.

Focus on expanding your belly, then the lungs. Feel your feet. Let the boots ground you.

Here, seventeen stories up, in a building built on a mountain, it was easy to feel as if there was no ground.

Selene rocked in the thick-soled boots. *Breathe in. Two. Three. Four.*

They watched Tabitha as they breathed. *Out. Two. Three. Four.*

Blond hair tangled around her face. She'd been sweating at some point. Her skin was so pale, with bright red dots on her cheeks.

Hectic. That's what Selene's mother used to call it.

Tabitha, lying there, inert on the cantilevered bed, stuck with tubes and surrounded by machines, should have looked quiet.

But she didn't. She looked as if her soul was off running a race somewhere. Or maybe she was panicking, trying to get some very important thing done.

Selene dropped their hand and walked toward Tabitha. A gray, padded chair sat near the head of the bed, angled just right to look at Tabitha's face. That was good. It meant people had been visiting, right?

Visitors were good.

Selene pulled out the chair and sat. They spent a moment finding their center. That place deep inside that acted as an internal compass when a person was in touch with it, and that waited, patiently, for the witch to return if they wandered off, astray.

Breathe in. Two. Three. Four.

The hospital sounds and smells didn't exactly recede. They just became less important as Selene focused on their inner landscape.

Drop your attention down. There. That place between navel and pelvis. *Breathe. Then open.*

Selene opened their awareness outward, seeking Tabitha's spirit. It felt so far away. They could definitely sense the panic. Some sort of battle was going on inside their friend.

Eyes open, but softly focused, Selene scanned Tabitha's ætheric body, the energy field closest to the skin, and then widened out to include her aura, the luminous body everyone carried around them. An egg-shaped sphere when a person was healthy, sometimes the aura looked like a cracked and shattered mirror. Other times it was misshapen, bumpy, a sure sign the person was trying to fit themselves into someone else, and the fit was not a good one.

Tabitha's ætheric body felt weakened. There was a brittleness about it, the way things got when they'd been battered too long and were trying to hold on. And the larger energy field of her aura?

Selene closed their eyes and tried to *see*. Not their strongest tool, but one they'd been working on.

Tabitha's aura was usually a bright, sunny thing, bursting with creative flow. A swirl of color and light, except for when she had a cold or something. Then things slowed down. But Selene had only ever encountered Tabitha slightly dimmed at worst.

This? It was as if someone had taken a brightly dyed cloth, and, before the dye had set, soaked it in a pail of water.

Tabitha's aura looked as if someone was slowly leeching her natural life force—and the life force she'd fought to build for herself—away.

"Damn it," Selene whispered into the sunlit room. They looked at their friend's face, at the too-pale skin, and those hectic dots. Tabitha was only half there. And now Selene knew why.

"Tabitha?" they murmured, leaning in close to her ear. "I'm going to try to help you. Please know it's me, Selene. Let me in."

Let me in so I can follow any traces I find, and then hunt this bastard down.

Selene placed a gentle hand on Tabitha's forehead, strengthening the link between them. And, amazingly, they felt a shift in Tabitha's ætheric field. As if it had softened, just a little. Welcoming Selene in.

Taking their hand away, Selene allowed their own spirit to enter Tabitha's energy field. Traveling into someone else's personal space was tricky, and Selene shouldn't have been doing it on their own. A voice in the back of their mind was screaming that they should wait. Call Brenda. Get an expert in here.

Selene slowed their breathing further, felt their ætheric body separate from their physical form...and flew.

They sent their spirit out and in and the same time, a thing they weren't even sure they knew how to do.

Focus. Breathe.

Tabitha's inner landscape was not what Selene would have expected. It looked as if someone had wandered through a cozy home, ripped down all the curtains, and stuck a knife into the cushions. There were traces of comfort and home. But mostly, it was all washed out. Bleached again. Scattered. Shattered.

And in the center of it all, Selene could feel Tabitha. Fighting. Struggling to hold on.

Where's the thread? Show me, Tabitha. What's doing this to you? A flash of rage spiked through Selene. Their fingers clenched.

Selene wanted to bust through doors and throttle whoever did this to Tabitha and Janice and who knew how many others. But they were inside Tabitha now. Tabitha deserved saving. Tabitha deserved their care.

Selene imagined turning a dial and slowing. Everything. Down. They needed to be careful here. Meticulous. Selene strengthened their connection to their core and called upon their ally and namesake to help them.

Guide me, Selene, Mother Moon. Help me see what Tabitha needs me to see.

Slowly. Carefully. Selene deepened their attention, then extended it three hundred and sixty degrees around. Where in the sacred circle that was Tabitha was the poison, or the threads that would lead Selene there?

Show me.

On the very edges of Selene's consciousness something vibrated.

The scent of tobacco.

Damn it.

Selene slowly turned, seeking through the washed-out colors, the destroyed sense of home. A smear of brown. And not the vital, humming, swaying brown of healthy tobacco leaves shining in the sun. Not the sweet, oily scent of tobacco being offered to the land.

No. Some magician had taken the spirit of the plant and chained it.

But there was something...else as well. Something. Where?

There.

Not just the resonance of tobacco. Not just a twined brown thread leading backwards to the thrice damned "alchemist."

It was something even worse. This alchemist had taken

sweet tobacco and made a servitor of it. A servitor was a magical servant, created only to do the work of the magician. They had no will of their own and could be fashioned for good or ill.

This poor creature—Selene could see it now—was a hunched and sniveling thing. One sliver of tobacco essence fought against the magic, but the rest? Fully chained.

And its only task was to seek out and poison brightness. Differentness. Art and music, love and joy. The poisoning itself was not the purpose though.

The purpose was this sick harnessing of life for the maker of the servitor.

The thick, twining brown rope wasn't just a link.

It was a conduit. A funnel. A siphon.

Shit. How much time do you have, Tabitha? How much time?

Selene nicked a slice in the rope and touched a finger there. Raising their finger to their mouth, Selene tasted the flow of Tabitha's life. Tasted her wild paintings and the way she loved to dance.

Tasted the poisonous nicotine she was bound to.

With a wave of their hand, Selene closed the slice.

Then began the process of withdrawing from Tabitha's spirit.

One step at a time.

18

JOSHUA

The day after the shop was closed was usually a good day in Joshua's book. He felt a bit less rushed, having had half a day off along with some time to catch up on bookkeeping, ordering, tidying, and all the other miscellany required to keep a retail business up and running.

Except his business wasn't running well. Only half of his distributors let him cancel his Faerie Fest order. The other half had already packed and shipped the items. It would cost him to return the stock, in more ways than one. Not only was there a return penalty, it undermined the good will he'd built up over the past several years.

And that bullshit "shamanism" teacher still had his blood boiling. It *had* to be this Alchemist asshole. They just couldn't prove it, yet.

Brenda thought they needed to call a grand coven of sorts, though Portland didn't have one. Basically, she thought they needed a meeting of all the magical organizations in the Portland metro area. The heathens. The OTO. The druids. The other witches. The head of the local Palo house.

Joshua had argued that they still needed more information. And that calling in a whole swathe of people was only going to make things take longer.

He and Brenda finally reached a compromise. If they weren't moving significantly forward in one week's time, she was going to start making calls.

Joshua quipped that she should just send out an e-vite. She'd given him a look he never wanted to see again.

He apologized. He wasn't usually an ass to people he respected, but this whole thing had him on edge. He also couldn't stop thinking about Selene and the fact that they were knee deep in all of this, and possibly in danger, made him very uneasy.

Joshua really wanted time to get to know Selene. Time to have fun. To date. To do things he hadn't wanted to do with someone in years, like eat breakfast, or climb Mount Tabor during spring.

He wandered through the shop, dusting shelves and putting books back into order. Reaching up to dust one of the fairies flying overhead, he heard the door open.

"Welcome to The Road Home!" he said, reaching for the second fairy wing. Then he turned.

There was a large man, white face ruddy, as if he had heart strain. Or imbibed more alcohol than was healthy for a person.

He just stood there, filling up the aisle. Out of place among the painted birch trees and the bright wish ribbons hanging from the branches closest to the door.

Oh, his clothing matched. It was as fanciful as the shop interior, and more fanciful even than Joshua's own.

A vest, half black, half white, buttoned over a peacock-blue shirt.

Albedo. Negredo. Cauda Pavonis.

Three of the alchemical stages. White. Black. Peacock. The Alchemist was here. What an ass. Oh, not that he was dressed like an alchemical dandy. That he advertised that he'd succeeded in his alchemy.

Knowing a little bit about just how difficult the alchemical process really was, Joshua truly doubted the man had achieved the peacock stage. He doubted he'd done much more than tinker in a lab, pretending.

Any fool could make a cup of coffee and call it alchemy.

It took a true practitioner to make the coffee good.

Damn it. Recognition must have shown on Joshua's face, because the man smiled, a broad rictus of a grin that made Joshua feel slightly ill.

"Greetings! I just thought I'd stop by. You didn't answer my note."

He stalked down the walkway, head turning, glancing at the contents of the shelves. He stopped when he got to the hand-blended oils. Sniffed.

"I don't see my ointment samples anywhere. I gave you so many, I thought you might have even succumbed to offering them for sale."

He looked at Joshua. The man was close enough now that Joshua could see that one ice-blue eye was bloodshot, and the other, clear.

A shiver ran down Joshua's back. He ignored it.

"What are you doing here?" Joshua asked, blocking the aisle. Thank the Gods no other customers were in the store, though he wished Quanice wasn't still sick. He could have used some backup.

The man—Joshua *really* didn't want to call him the Alchemist—looked around the displays again. Picked up a brown glass tester vial of Choose Love, looked at the label and sneered.

"How sweet. Choose Love." He set the vial back down and trained the ice-blue eyes back on Joshua. "I would think that a young man like you would want to choose power. Or knowledge. Or immortality. Or something more interesting."

What are you, Faust? Joshua thought.

The man traced one finger down a bookcase, coming closer. "Though I suppose love is potent enough for magic, if you use it right. Do you?"

"Do I what?"

"Use other people's love to fuel your magic. That's what the best gurus do, you know. Raise all that love energy and just eat it down." The man raised his fingers to his mouth, and mimed chomping on a sandwich. "Yum yum yum."

The basics again. Feet. Breath. Spine. Center. Hands.

Joshua imagined he could connect to the earth beneath the shop. Past the city services and down into soil. And further still, to the iron core of the earth itself. He willed the energy upward, filling himself with chthonic power.

Then he raised his hands. Felt the energy pooling in his palms. A warning. A warding.

"What. Do. You. Want."

The ruddy-faced man stopped. Shrugged. Lifted his hands and shook them in the air, as if to say he meant no harm. That he was simply an innocent person who had wandered into Joshua's store.

"I simply came by to see if you enjoyed my gift. And to ask if you knew of any place I could teach a few classes." The man paused. "My living room is simply growing too small. I had *no idea* there would be this kind of interest in my small offerings. It turns out that a lot of middle class people want a taste of the exotic."

Joshua's vision flashed black, then white, then resolved

itself again. Rage. Blinding rage. He couldn't succumb. He breathed and straightened up his spine, feeling his feet sink slightly into the floorboards. Joshua stood as tall as he could.

"Get out of my store," he said.

The man gave a little half smile and shrugged again.

The door to the shop opened, and a parent holding her small child's hand trundled in.

Joshua stepped toward the man and lowered his voice to a whisper. "Get out of my store. Now."

"Well!" The man took a step back. "Thank you for your help. But this sort of oil is not what I need. He placed the Choose Love tester back on the shelf and turned.

The woman crouched next to the child, pointing at some glass-cased faerie statues.

"Excuse me," the man said, skirting around them.

The woman barely looked up, then turned her attention back to the toddler who babbled who knew what.

The door opened. Shut. The Alchemist was gone.

Joshua gave his hands a subtle shake and took in what felt like the first normal breath in an hour. The whole exchange must have only taken five minutes, but felt much longer.

You've got to get back in shape, man.

Joshua willed a smile onto his face and picked up his feather duster.

"Welcome to The Road Home. Let me know if I can show you anything. We've got some soft toys and children's books on the shelves just to your left."

The woman smiled up at him with big brown eyes. Normal eyes. Beautiful eyes.

Just a human, trying to share a bit of magic with her child.

Joshua palmed the vial of Choose Love and slipped it in his pocket. It was tainted now.

He would dispose of it properly later.

19

SELENE

Selene sat on a plump cushion inside the permanent circle in Raquel's attic. Raquel had supplemented the house AC with a portable unit, so at least it was blessedly cool.

They were tired. There never seemed to be enough time to even eat, let alone sleep.

Selene felt singed around the edges, and they were nowhere near through. Not for the day, and likely not for some time. All they wanted to do was crawl into bed and stay there for a week.

But once the cascade of events started, they knew, there was never rest until the magic was either done or had unwound itself. Not that anything was ever fully complete, either. But things had a way of at least being "done for now."

That now had not arrived.

Raquel's attic had been home to many intense rituals. The slanted, creamy white ceiling carried powerful energy signatures of all the workings the coven had done over the years. The shelves set into the knee walls held all the external tools of those workings. Everything a witch could need to boost and focus what was inside herself.

Selene felt all of those workings, reaching down to the dark stain on the broad Douglas fir planks scattered with bright cushions, cycling back up to the vee of the ceiling. Workings of joy and laughter, sorrow and grief, and rituals to take down the people who meant others harm.

That last was turning out to be Selene's specialty. One they never would have thought they could have borne, not in their wildest childhood dreams. The dreams where they got back at everyone who had ever bullied anyone, or put them on drugs that made them feel sluggish and stole away their imaginations, or...

Oh, Selene had read the books, just like so many other small, nerdy, bullied children. The one where a magical horse showed up to tell you that you were so special, so hurting and misunderstood, that they were taking you away to someplace better. The ones where wardrobes opened onto what should have been real life. A life where things were never boring, and what the children did actually mattered. Books that told Selene they could ride dragons, and be brave, and go into battle to save their town.

But Selene's magic felt like a burden lately. As if they were filled with nothing but darkness, and the need to strike things down.

But what if? What if Selene really was the child destined to save their city?

Raquel set fat beeswax pillars in the center, surrounding some flakes of tobacco. Their anchor to the damn liquid nicotine poisoning their friends.

"Are you ready?" Raquel asked, breaking into Selene's reverie. Selene blinked and looked at the others, sitting on floor cushions just like their own, forming a rough oval on the attic floor.

Tobias. Brenda. Tempest. Moss. No Alejandro or Lucy. They couldn't make it on such short notice. Their places were taken by Legis, who was somehow connected to this. He held a big-ass sword that glimmered in the light filtering through the attic windows. Selene had no idea why.

Told to bring it, was all he had said. And that sort of thing was never good. Right?

And then there was Joshua. With his warm red lips peeking from the middle of his goatee. With his warm brown eyes. His cream, open-collared shirt and gray linen waistcoat. Gorgeous.

And Selene felt that nervous sweat again, despite the AC. Damn it.

Maybe your body is telling you to take a chance? they thought.

Couldn't be it. Why would Joshua be interested in Selene, anyway?

"You ready?" Raquel asked, breaking Selene from their reverie.

"Not really." Selene gave a little sigh. "But we've got to do this. And I'm the only one with an in to the poor servitor that nasty man constructed."

"Wait a minute," Joshua said. "I just thought of something."

He rocked to one side, reaching into the right pocket of his black trousers, pulling out a small, brown glass vial. "He touched this. Held it for a couple minutes."

Holding it out, he leaned toward Selene. Their fingers touched his palm as Selene lifted it gingerly, only touching the black cap. His palm was warm.

Selene exhaled, then tried to tune into the vial. There

was definitely *something* around it. And it felt unsettlingly familiar.

"What do you think?" they asked, turning first to Brenda, then Tobias. "I wish Lucy was here."

"We should be able to use it as a focus," Brenda said. "It might even help me follow you in, if necessary. If nothing else, it'll help the rest of us stay centered on the Alchemist."

Having a focus was good, though Selene still wasn't sure what the hell they were going to do once they found the servitor again. Selene placed the vial in the center of the space, smack in the middle of the candles.

"Remember," Tobias said, placing a hand on Selene's shoulder, "this is just reconnaissance. We just need more information. Don't go all hotdog on us."

"When have I ever 'gone hotdog?'"

"Ahem." Tempest fake-cleared her throat. "Like that time you were just supposed to push the Nazis out of the park, but set them on fire instead?"

Selene grinned at that, then shook out their hands. There was too much energy gathering and nowhere to put it. And Joshua was sitting way too close for comfort.

Selene could smell him. Today he wore some mixture of sandalwood and cedar, topped with a high note of rose. Selene wanted to bite him, right where his neck met his starched collar.

Instead, they inhaled and tried to return to center. This magical operation was no joke. They sent a quick thought to the moon, just barely waning. It was still full enough to be a strong ally for the work ahead.

The sun, too, Selene supposed. But they really weren't ready for that much brightness yet.

Raquel lit the candles. Tempest snapped her fingers in the four cardinal directions, then above and below.

Selene felt the wards that protected the space flare, then activate themselves with a low, pulsing hum.

Funny, Selene didn't usually sense things like that so clearly. Something was changing, but there was no time to think about that now. They adjusted themselves, feet on the floor, knees supported by the cushion. Spine rising freely from their pelvis. Head aligned on top of spine.

"I'm ready," Selene said. Then sent their spirit out, following the scent of tobacco, and a thick, twining rope of energy, hopefully leading to the servitor.

20

JOSHUA

He looked across the circle at Legis. The Thelemite seemed surprisingly unperturbed, though there was no way this was his usual magical jam. The man sat, stoic on his cushion. Solid. Just waiting to be called upon if there was need. It made Joshua realize just how little he actually knew about the man. Maybe it was time to change that. Become actual friends with some people again.

Joshua knew Arrow and Crescent worked like this all the time, though he'd only been party to one of their magical operations once before, and that was more as a bystander, though he'd done his best in the moment.

He'd actually acted as if he was a man who still worked magic then. As if he hadn't abdicated his will to disillusionment, drinking and dancing and sexing his way through the local Goth scene.

Arrow and Crescent did that to people, though. They brought the best and strongest out of you, regardless of what you thought of yourself.

So here he was, back to basics with people who had real

mastery. He just hoped when it was time to throw down, he didn't mess things up.

Selene looked almost ethereal, sitting tall on their own cushion. Damn, they were gorgeous. Raquel had moved him across the circle from Selene, saying that since he'd had the only actual physical sighting of the man, that he and Selene needed to balance out the circle, not consolidate at one quadrant.

Whatever that meant. But it made some sort of intuitive sense. The two strongest connections to the Alchemist needed to have a clear path to each other across the space.

His eyes traced the contours of Selene's face. The high cheekbones. Their dark eyes, closed now. The lips, only lightly painted today, in a ruddy shade of plum. On down to the soft rise and fall of their chest beneath an open-necked black shirt. Collarbones. Silver necklace with a silver skull pendant.

Selene's skin had a slight tinge of what some people called "olive," making Joshua wonder where their people had come from, generations ago.

Selene gave a slight shudder. Joshua could almost feel them as they began to travel, tracing the path of the brown tobacco rope they said was inside of Tabitha. The one Selene had cut, and tasted.

Oh, and hadn't that pissed off Tobias and Raquel.

"You've just put yourself in danger of magical poisoning! Or worse!" Tobias had actually shouted at Selene. Selene had held firm. It was their magic, and they knew what they were doing. So badass.

Joshua's gaze rested on the brown glass vial in the center of the flickering candles. He could almost see a faint miasma rising from the surface of the glass. That was strange. The swirling energy seemed to be increasing.

He looked at Selene again. They seemed so far away. Brows creased.

Selene frowned. Something was wrong. He tried to tune into them more closely. Tried to sense what they sensed. See what they saw.

Closing his own eyes, he slowed his breathing down. Tried to remember what it felt like to leave his body. To let his spirit travel on the æthers. Joshua could hear his heartbeat, as loud as if he held a stethoscope to his chest. His body felt heavy. His head pulsed and hummed. *Up and out,* he thought.

Buoyancy. Lightness. Slipping out the crown of his head, Joshua found himself floating above the room, bouncing up near the apex of the attic ceiling.

He saw the circle. Everyone's unique smudge of color and vibration. He saw Selene, saw the shimmering cord connecting soul to body. Saw the road they traveled.

Saw Selene facing what looked like a small, desiccated little brown being. Stubby arms and legs. Squat feet and face. It looked as if energy was passing between them. As if they were having some sort of communication.

Nothing to help with. He pulled his vision back to the room itself. Down to the central space. The candles. The...

Joshua was looking at the vial. It glowed. Oh shit. A swirling miasma reached out, headed toward Selene's body. The Alchemist must have booby-trapped the vial.

Wrenching his consciousness back into his body, Joshua lurched, instant headache spiking through his skull.

"Tobias!" Joshua shouted. "Do something! Legis! Protect Selene! The Alchemist! He's coming to get them!"

Joshua flung his body at the center of the circle, scattering candles. One of them tipped, extinguishing itself.

Raquel's strong brown hand wrapped around his wrist.

"Don't touch that," she said, voice flat.

"But..."

Legis lifted his sword, and plunged it point down in between Selene and the vial.

The energy snapped; the brown vial shattered, shards flying. Selene rocked on their cushion. Joshua ripped his wrist from Raquel's grip, and, knocking aside the rest of the candles, held out his arms.

A nasty *crunch*. Sharp pain in his left knee. The glass.

And then Selene was in his arms, shaking, his head was screaming, and he was easing them down onto the cushions, barely aware of Raquel cursing as she stomped the edges of a smoldering cushion.

Moss and Tempest were doing something. Something important... The circle. It had to... remain solid. Protect.

The pain in his head spiked. Joshua's sight went gray, then black. He felt Selene, solid in his arms.

Then nothing.

21

SELENE

Raquel had tucked Selene up on one end of the overstuffed red living room couch, with Brenda at the other end to keep an eye on them. If it hadn't still been eighty degrees outside, Selene swore Raquel would have wrapped them up in a throw, too. Joshua was ensconced in one of the chairs flanking the impressive fireplace, dressed in a bathrobe that clearly came from Raquel's new boyfriend, Charlie. It swamped Joshua's thin frame.

Huh. The robe must mean Charlie was sleeping over, and that Raquel's son, Zion, must be cool with it.

"Where's Zion, anyway?" Selene asked, still groggy from the magical backlash. They'd been yanked from the æthers by Tobias. That was never fun. Could have been worse though, and was, from the looks of Joshua, who had passed out from the pain of it.

Tempest was doing some sort of energy healing work, focused on Joshua's head. His color was slowly returning, but he still didn't look so great, a little sweaty despite the air conditioning. There were dark pouches beneath his closed eyes. He looked a little like something that wandered in from a children's fairy tale, and not one of the nice ones.

Selene should have given Joshua the couch. He was clearly in a lot worse shape than they were.

Apparently Joshua had gone astral traveling without warning, then slammed back into his body when he figured out Selene was in danger. That sort of thing always left a headache, and sometimes nausea, too. You wanted to exit and enter the body very slowly, in a measured way. That was what coven training had taught Selene. And Selene had no idea how thorough Joshua's training had been. They had a feeling he was one of those scattershot, auto-didact, half-trained people with a lot of natural talent.

Nothing wrong with that, except when it exacted a steep price.

And magic always exacted *some* price, whether the witch or magician was aware of it or not.

Magic could be tricky, even in the best trained people's hands.

Selene was thinking of the servitor. It turned out it didn't particularly *like* being a servitor. The Alchemist had messed up.

A servitor was basically magical AI. Creating a servitor —at least what Selene had studied, they'd never done it themself—required the magician to infuse it with a certain amount of intelligence. Too much, and it could develop its own ideas, and maybe even, eventually, its own will.

Despite being a creation of the Alchemist, this servitor had somehow decided it was more strongly aligned to the spirit of tobacco than to the man who made it. Probably because tobacco was the food the Alchemist was giving it. You always had to feed a servitor something to keep it going. Tobacco was the obvious choice here.

Selene bet the Alchemist had no idea the servitor was gaining in autonomy. That could prove useful. At least they hoped so.

Anything they could use to track the dangerous idiot and stop him from poisoning more people, the better.

Goddess. Poor Janice. No way did she deserve to die because this idiot had some who-knows-what plan. Or was just a psychopath who decided magic was a great way to control people.

Meanwhile, Tobias sat on an ottoman, carefully picking tiny glass shards out of Joshua's knee. They'd had to cut his lovely trousers off—hence the robe—because there was no good way to take the pants off and get to the wound without grinding the glass in further. Joshua hissed periodically.

Moss came into the room, carrying a brown bottle of hydrogen peroxide, along with a tube of antiseptic and some gauze. He set them on the coffee table and grabbed a chair.

Legis sat silently on the floor and watched. Selene didn't see his sword. They wanted to ask about it but were too tired.

"What are we going to do about those classes he's teaching?" Raquel asked. She set a bottle of wine on the table, along with some glasses, then flopped down in the other chair, corkscrew in hand. "In my mind, that's almost as dangerous as the tainted flying ointment. Yemọja knows what he's doing with those people."

Raquel worked the corkscrew into the bottle of Oregon Pinot, and waggled the bottle first at Brenda, then at Selene.

"I'll take a splash," Brenda said, and then looked at Selene. "I'm not sure you should have any."

"Is there any iced tea?" Selene asked. Brenda was right. Alcohol was the last thing they needed.

Raquel started to rise. Moss waived her back.

"I'll get it," he said.

"Who *is* this guy, anyway?" Tobias asked. "I mean, where'd he come from? Has he been hiding out somewhere, doing his own thing? Did he just move here?"

Brenda tapped a ringed finger on her wineglass. Selene followed her gaze. Her eyes were trained on the amazing oil portrait of a young Zion as the Tarot card The Sun. A young Black boy, carefree and smiling, running arms upraised, surrounded by golden light.

Illumination. There was something about it Selene would pay attention to if only their head wasn't filled with cotton wool. Something...damn it. Exposure. Too much light. They still wanted to retreat to their favored velvety darkness, lit only by stars and the light of the moon.

But the world kept telling them to step into the sun and be seen.

"If you read cards or runes, or use astrology," Raquel had told Selene early on, *"you can also learn to read the patterns right in front of you. In your self. And in your life."*

Well fuck. This was a pattern emerging, wasn't it?

"What I wonder is why?" Brenda was asking. "What's his end game? What is he trying to achieve?"

Moss came back in with a clinking, blue-glazed pottery pitcher of iced tea and some glasses on a tray. Brenda leaned forward and moved wineglasses to make space on the coffee table.

"Who cares?" Moss said. He set the tray down with a thunk that caused the tea to slosh in the pitcher. "He's an asshole who wants a taste of power and is getting it by abusing people. His endgame is probably just to feel like he's the king."

"That's it." Tobias and Selene spoke simultaneously.

Selene had spoken out of some inner sense of rightness,

but couldn't articulate why.

Tobias dabbed at Joshua's knee with the hydrogen peroxide, then secured gauze over it with medical tape. Selene just waited, hoping Joshua would chime in.

Tobias set aside the tape and extra gauze and poured himself a glass of tea. Moss jerked, seeming to recall why he'd brought the pitcher in the first place. Moss poured a second glass and handed it to Selene with an apologetic smile.

Selene nodded a thanks and smiled back.

"He really wanted me to be cowed and frightened. Or even angry." Joshua's voice sounded raspy and far away, as though he was still halfway on the astral. No wonder he hadn't been chiming in. He was barely in the room.

Brenda noticed. "Someone grab Joshua's feet."

Tobias set his tea down and grasped Joshua's ankles, then placed the palms of his hands on the tops of Joshua's feet. He would be pressing downward, while simultaneously imagining Joshua's spirit filling his whole body.

"Joshua," Brenda continued. "Imagine drawing your spirit all the way down to your toes. Follow Tobias's energy, okay? Breathe deeply, and fill your body all the way back up again."

Joshua heaved in a huge breath, then coughed, shuddering slightly. Then his breathing evened out, deepening. More color returned to his skin. He started looking more like a handsome dandy and less like a night hag.

He opened his brown eyes. They had a golden tinge Selene had never noticed before. Brown and gold, like a tiger's eyes. A dapper, slender tiger.

"Thanks," he said, voicing sounding a bit more solid. "Tea?"

Moss poured him a glass. Tobias handed it over.

Joshua's hand shook slightly, ice clinking in the glass as he drank.

He coughed again, then spoke. "What I meant to say is, the man just wanted a reaction, to prove he was controlling me. That's what Moss meant by king, I think. That the Alchemist wants to know everyone he encounters falls under his thrall, just because he wills it."

"Well, this Black woman isn't making anyone her king, let alone a white man. So what are we going to do about this asshole?" Raquel said.

Everyone fell silent for a moment.

Selene took another sip of tea. Thinking, like everyone else in the room. Joshua closed his eyes, resting his head on the back of the chair. A lock of dark hair fell over his forehead. Selene wanted to stroke it back into place.

No time for that right now.

"I think his servitor isn't completely under his control. And it certainly doesn't seem to like him much," Selene said.

Every head but Joshua's snapped their way.

Brenda and Raquel nodded.

"That's good. Very good," Raquel said.

"So, how do we convince the servitor it's in its best interests to help us?" Moss asked.

"That's what we need to work on, isn't it?" Selene replied.

And they had no idea how. Or if any of these vague ideas were even going to work.

A voice rumbled from the corner. Legis. Selene had almost forgotten he was even there.

"First, we need to figure out what exactly the servitor's task is. If its only job is funneling life energy from the poisoned people to this Alchemist ass, we can probably just figure out how to interrupt the flow. It's more complex than that, but that's a good starting point." He scooted forward and snagged the wine bottle and a glass. While Legis poured the ruby liquid, Moss spoke.

"What other kind of tasks could it have? I've never worked with servitors. Sigils are more my bag."

Legis drank, then swirled the glass in one big hand. "Good question. I'm not one-hundred percent convinced he's using the little guy to funnel energy. Or, that may just a by-product. There has to be something else going on. But I'm going to need to meditate on it for a few days."

"Do you think we have a few days?" Selene asked.

"You'd know that more than I would," Legis replied. "All I know is we don't currently have answers, but they feel close. I suggest we sit here and enjoy this wine, and stop trying so hard."

Selene nodded.

Legis sipped some more, then spoke again.

"Every magical working requires both effort and integration. To Know. To Will. To Dare. To Keep Silence. They need to cycle. If we let this rest in silence for a while, we should cycle back to the power To Know."

Selene rattled the melting ice in their glass. "I think I'm ready for some wine now." Brenda shot them a look.

"Just half a glass," Selene protested. Moss was already pouring.

Moss handed them the wine, exchanging it for the now empty tumbler.

"Hey Legis," Moss asked. "Didn't Crowley add a fifth power to that formula?"

Legis smiled. "He did indeed. He said when all of Éliphas Lévi's four powers were activated, they formed a fifth. He called it the power To Go."

22

———

JOSHUA

Joshua felt so beaten up, he had taken a car service to work. He felt grateful he had enough money to text a Lyft instead of having to navigate the jostling of the bus.

"Thank you," he said to the woman who'd been kind enough to drive him to the shop in exchange for money.

"Have a great day, now!" Her bright accent was distinctly not from the Pacific Northwest.

Climbing out of the car with a groan, Joshua was also grateful he'd had the presence of mind to get dropped in front of the coffee shop attached to the Hawthorne bookshop instead of The Road Home. He sighed, and hoisted his black leather purse more firmly on his shoulder. The shop would wait another ten minutes.

Thank the Gods Quanice was feeling better. Joshua had called him and asked if he could open the shop, which meant coming in half an hour before it was set to open. Quanice readily agreed, which meant Joshua had been able to soak in an epsom salt bath, get slowly dressed, and have a cup of coffee before heading out the door.

At least Joshua's brain was a little more clear, despite the lingering headache. He had been too out of it the night before to remember that chaos magicians used servitors all the time. They used them to help buy a little extra time when needed. They used them to help them study—though why they couldn't just design a simple sigil for that, Joshua wasn't sure. There was way too much he didn't know about this stuff.

Another reason he needed to get serious again. A, his shop needed serious magical help along with a physical plane revamp, if it was going to survive. And B, if he kept getting dragged into messed-up situations like this, he might as well be of better use. If he reached the edges of his slap-dash training and innate power, he was rapidly going to become a liability.

He pushed open the glass door, which felt heavy as lead, and wound his way past the bookstore portion, back toward the café.

Point being, Quanice was a Gods-blessed *chaos magician.* If Joshua's head wasn't still pounding, he would have slapped his forehead at the stupidity of it. He should have brought Quanice into this days ago. If he didn't have the chops himself, he'd know someone who did.

If the shop wasn't busy, he'd be able to talk to Quanice in between customers.

Joshua wanted one of the bookstore's breakfast sandwiches. A load of protein and carbs was just what he needed right now. English muffin surrounding egg, cheddar, and bacon, all baked together in one flat round.

Louise, a gray-haired white woman with purple cat-eye glasses, smiled at him as he walked to the counter. He was certain he was hobbling.

"What can I get you today, Joshua?"

"Two large coffees, one with extra cream. And two breakfast sandwiches, please."

Louise placed his order and rang him up.

"It'll be up in a jiff."

As he waited, he perused the corkboard bristling with business cards, glossy club cards, and a few old fashioned 8x11 fliers. One enterprising local author had left club cards with book covers on the fronts. He smiled. Good advertising.

Maybe The Road Home needed to paper the other neighborhoods with fliers. He wondered what the rate of return was on those. There had to be some way to get the word out they were here.

Maybe he needed a night class in marketing or something. Gah. Being a shop owner was complicated enough, without having to study all this other stuff. But if he was going to stay afloat, and keep both the store and his home, he had to do something.

These were the perils of trying to be a responsible early thirties adult. Most days he didn't envy his age cohort. He knew it was a struggle for everyone. But days like today? He sometimes wished he just worked for someone else and lived in a house with four other people.

But that only seemed simpler and appealing for about thirty seconds.

Joshua sighed. He had to step up his spiritual practice. He had to step up his business game. What else?

You know the answer to that, his snarky inner self replied.

Yeah. Eventually he was going to need to step up his relationship game. Stop hiding from the stuff he'd buried after Jessie was killed.

What the...?

There on the corkboard was another one of those fliers Moss had found. The mash-up of "shamanism" and "alchemy." As if it was either. It was made to sound all spooky and sexy, designed to draw people in. It made him feel a little sick.

He looked more closely.

"Joshua, your order's up!"

Ignoring the summons, he peered more closely at the flier. This version had a symbol chasing itself around the edges. He ripped the flier off the board, grabbed the coffees and sandwiches, thanked Louise, and somehow managed to open the heavy door.

A skateboarder narrowly avoided him. "Sorry, man!"

Joshua vaguely recognized the guy. Maybe he studied with Brenda? Balancing his load, he turned the corner and managed to make it the one block to the shop, whose orange door and leafy window displays beckoned.

Everything felt as if it was taking too long this morning. And he just realized that the shop door had a knob to open, and he had no hands, and was afraid to juggle everything into one arm in his current condition. He could just see everything crashing to the sidewalk, coffee staining his brand new tan linen trousers and matching waistcoat.

So he kicked the door and waited. Then kicked again.

The door swung open, and Quanice peeked out, clearly wondering what the hell was going on.

"Oh my Gods, man! You okay? You look like shit!" Quanice, never tactful, was at least kind and perceptive, and immediately unburdened Joshua of the cardboard coffee holder and the bag of breakfast.

"Thanks for the compliment, Quanice."

"Oh. Sorry. I didn't mean..."

"No. It's fine. Let's just get this in."

They walked into the cool, serene aura of the store. Quanice had put some ambient electronica with an interesting beat onto the store system. It married nicely with the fountain that burbled quietly by the door.

"Any customers?" Joshua asked, as he followed Quanice toward the long counter at the end of the shop. He saw that Quanice had been pricing pendulums. Good.

"Not right now. Had a few in earlier. One lady bought a stack of books, a pendulum, and the Urban Tarot deck."

"Nice."

That was good to hear. Big sales like that made all the difference to the bottom line.

"I need to talk to you about some magic. Why don't we talk while we eat?"

"Sounds good to me," Quanice said, setting the food on the counter and clearing the pendulums away.

Joshua spread the flier out. "First question. Do you recognize this sigil?" He pointed to the running pattern around the edge of the paper.

Quanice sipped at his coffee as he examined the shapes. "It isn't a symbol in common use, if that's what you're asking. At least not that I've encountered. But..."

The young man traced the shapes, mouth half-forming words as he did.

He stopped, lifted his finger from the paper and said, "Well, fuck me."

"What?"

Quanice slid the paper closer to Joshua and pointed. "Look here. It's words. Two words. See the interlocking letters?"

Joshua brought the paper closer to his face. Was he going to have to start wearing glasses?

He saw what Quanice meant, though. The shapes were letter-like. But he still couldn't make out the words.

"You see the words in here? What are they?"

Quanice swallowed his coffee. "The classics," he said. "Sex." He pointed. "Will."

Joshua looked again. "I still don't see it."

Quanice leaned against the counter for a moment, sipping his coffee and thinking.

"Are you familiar with Arabic at all?"

"Some."

"There's a calligraphic form called 'square kufic' that turns Arabic words into interlocking patterns. It's really beautiful, and used a lot for prayers, or to illustrate the ninety-nine names of God."

He set his coffee down and grabbed a scrap of paper and pen from one of the counter drawers. "Look what he's done here. He's squaring off the letters, combining them, and reversing some directions so they fit into a tight pattern. It's not nearly as elegant as kufic, but it works for his purposes."

Quanice drew a square S, and then, in the bottom half, he drew a leftward facing line. "See? That's the reverse E embedded in the original S."

"What's the thing that looks like a rune in the middle?"

A huge grin on his face, Quanice smacked one hand on the wooden counter. Joshua winced. Still a bit too loud for his head.

"That's the thing that had me fooled for a minute. He repeated that X shape in order to draw the line down the center, forming both the W and an I. That forms a T bar at the bottom that stands in for mirrored Ls. And the S begins again. Pretty well done, actually."

Joshua stared at the pattern. Sex and Will. Life force and intention harnessed toward action. Two concepts that acted as building blocks for almost every magical operation in the Western world.

"Okay. So I get that. But what are they doing *here*?"

Quanice rustled in the bag and drew out their sandwiches.

He gave Joshua one of those "you're my boss so I'm too polite to say what I *really* think looks."

Setting his sandwich down with a sigh, Quanice said, "Look. If you were a charlatan, or a megalomaniac, or psychopath..."

"Or all three."

"Or all three," Quanice nodded. "You would want to draw unsuspecting people into your working by promising their subconscious minds the very thing you want to use them for."

He picked up a sandwich, took a bite, and chewed.

Joshua took a drink of his coffee with extra cream, waiting for Quanice to stop stalling for effect.

"So if you want to prey on people, using them as batteries or psychic cannon fodder or whatever, you slide in subliminal messages. Trap set."

"Well, isn't *that* unscrupulous."

Quanice swallowed a second bite.

"Yeah, sure. But we do it, too. We just say we mean well. You turn the fountain on every morning. We've got nice faeries flying overhead. We're telegraphing to people that we have what they want, and maybe even what they need. It's basic marketing. And basic psychology."

"Quanice, if I could afford it, I'd offer you a raise."

Quanice just smiled and shrugged.

"So what's your second question?" Quanice asked.

"Oh! Right! Well, now there's a third. First, can you brainstorm some marketing ideas for the shop, since you're so savvy? And meanwhile, can you tell me everything you know about servitors?"

23

SELENE

Selene was so far behind on work, it wasn't funny. But they couldn't get Tabitha out of their head, so here they were, back at the hospital again, despite the fact that the smells and lighting made their skin crawl.

Tabitha's parents had been in the room when Selene arrived. A white couple in their mid-fifties, they looked exhausted, and seemed slightly relieved to have an excuse to take a break and get some food.

Staring at your grown child, inert on a bed, when there wasn't a damn thing you could do to help them must be horrible. Selene had assured the couple that they'd stay put for at least an hour. To take a break. Get out the hospital if they could.

So here Selene sat, in the gray padded chair, listening to the hissing and beeping machines, staring down at Tabitha's face.

She looked even worse than the day before. More sunken. Less present.

"You bastard," Selene muttered.

They still couldn't imagine how anyone could bear to

do magic that sucked other people's life away. The coven had done some tracking, and saw how he was doing it, but they still didn't know some major things. And not knowing major things meant that any magic Arrow and Crescent might try to do to counter this mess would most likely fail.

They couldn't just fire at random. Nor could they simply trace the threads back to the source and blast the guy. Not without knowing whether or not that would harm who knew how many other people were keyed into him. Not only the people he had poisoned, but his so-called "students" who were most likely just more cannon fodder, along with being his bankroll.

They also didn't know why he was doing this, and frankly, they didn't know how. Setting magical tags inside people's auras was a pretty simple operation if you actually knew what you were doing, and knew how to avoid getting messed up in the process.

But tagging the flying ointment? And including poison? The two things seemed counterintuitive. It seemed like you were either just an asshole who got off on poisoning people, or you wanted to syphon juice from them.

And it was just a numbers game? Or something else besides?

Maybe the Alchemist didn't care how many casualties there were, as long as some people were strong enough to survive and do whatever nasty working he had planned.

Selene texted Brenda. The coven had to make sure that Lucy hadn't gotten tagged when they touched the goop.

Then they sighed. There was no way to protect anyone in the labs, was there? Hopefully whatever magical nasties he'd hidden along with the poison couldn't pass through nitrile gloves.

"Tabitha, I wish you could tell me what's happening to you...."

Selene just didn't have the juice to go into their friend's aura again. Not today.

Body trumps spirit, Raquel always said. And both Selene's body and spirit needed some rest and repair. But what Selene *could* do was brainstorm.

They couldn't stop thinking about what Legis had said the night before. About the Power To Go. This magic felt so convoluted. Complicated. The bad guy had entangled all of these innocent people, not just in his actions, but in his magic.

How in Goddess's name was the coven supposed to help?

Legis's comment was as good a starting place as any. They needed to go back through all of the Four Powers, it seemed, in order to find the right action. To Go would only follow after the rest of the work was done.

Clicking open a fresh page on their tablet, Selene decided to make a list.

To Know, they headed the first section.

What *did* they know?

The Alchemist was poisoning flying ointment.

The same person was also teaching classes in "shaman-ism" and "alchemy."

Random people were seizing. Some had died. How many, the coven didn't know yet. They also didn't know how many others were in Tabitha's state, or had come through somehow and were being used regardless.

They also didn't know what exactly this man was doing with his students.

Most importantly? They didn't know his endgame or how the flying ointment was tagging people. Maybe Tobias or Brenda could figure that out. They couldn't ask Lucy right now...which was a drag. Their best psychometrist was compromised. They'd have to rely strictly on the herbs or would need to find an energy signature some other way.

Good thing Joshua still had a box of the stuff in his storeroom.

Okay. Moving on.

To Will.

So far, their intention was to find out what the Alchemist was doing, and to protect whomever they could. But how to set that into action? And could they even plan an action with so little information?

Selene looked at Tabitha, who seemed to be hanging on to her spirit by the slimmest silver thread.

They were going to have to plan an action, and fill in the information as they went.

So. First steps? Use the ties they *did* have to do more reconnaissance. Maybe the coven needed to track down some of this guy's students, see if there were any inroads from that direction.

The power to Dare. Selene didn't like this one at all. Not in this situation. Usually, Selene was all for leaping off the cliff in the name of righteous action. But this time? That worry about casualties was strong.

They sighed again and looked at the machines that seemed to fill the room. Bringing the stylus up against their lips, they tried to think. Selene closed their eyes and took in a deep breath.

Despite saying they weren't going to, they sent a tendril of awareness toward Tabitha. Reaching out. Seeking.

Tell me... they asked her sleeping form.

And felt a shiver in response. Felt a tugging at their own

aura. So slight, they would have missed it if they hadn't been paying full attention.

"We're connected, aren't we?" they whispered into the *sshhing*, beeping room.

But was the connection from their friendship, or because of *him*?

Selene tried to scan their own aura, something they had learned how to do when they first joined Arrow and Crescent coven. Today it felt hard. They were too tired. Shouldn't even be attempting this.

To Dare.

:Selene?:

Tabitha? Selene set their tablet aside and reached for Tabitha's closest hand, avoiding the pulse oximeter on her finger. *Are you there?*

Was that a squeeze? Yes. Selene thought it was.

Hang on, Tabitha. We're trying to help you! Your parents are here and...

:So far away...scared. He's bleeding me. Us.:

Selene knew that, but feeling the information from Tabitha somehow made it worse. The bed railing dug into their arm. They didn't care.

Do you know why? Probably too much to ask, but it was one of the most important questions Selene had.

:Taking...trying...to prove...:

Selene could feel Tabitha straining. Trying to form concepts into words. They looked for the cord that tethered Tabitha to her body. It had grown even thinner. This was so messed up.

And Selene didn't have any juice to give her.

"We're back," a soft voice said from the door. Selene kept hold of Tabitha's hand and turned their head.

"Hey," Selene said.

The parents looked slightly better. Their faces were still creased with worry, but the food and air must have done them some good.

Maybe Tabitha's parents had some life force to give.

"Um...I think she squeezed my hand," Selene said.

Tabitha's father stepped closer. "Really? That's good. I mean, right?"

Selene nodded. Then they squeezed Tabitha's hand and sent out another thought.

I'm going to try to help you. Your parents are back now. Hang on, okay?

Selene stood.

"I read a study that said talking to your loved ones and holding their hands can sometimes bring people out of comas."

Selene didn't know if that was true but figured there must have been a study like that, somewhere.

They cleared their throat and shuffled their feet back and forth before forcing themself to stop again.

"The article said that they can feel the presence of family and friends. So I was holding Tabitha's hand, talking, and trying to send her love, you know?"

Tabitha's mother nodded. Her father wiped his eyes with a white handkerchief.

"Then that's just what we'll do," he said, folding the handkerchief back into a square and replacing it in his rear jeans pocket. "We'll take turns holding her hand, and sending love."

"May as well try," her mother said. "Nothing the hospital is doing seems to work."

Selene gathered up their tablet, making room near the bed. Shoving their things back into the messenger bag, they headed for the door.

"It was really nice meeting you. I'll be back. And if you need anything, please call."

"Thank you so much for everything," Tabitha's mother said, then turned toward her daughter again.

Selene just hoped whatever love they sent her would be enough to keep Tabitha's spirit anchored here.

The coven still needed more time to figure this out.

Selene hoped Tabitha would make it.

24

——————

JOSHUA

Joshua was on the 14 bus heading to the Mercado to meet Legis and Frater Louis for dinner.

The shop had done pretty good business after the little breakfast-and-magical-theory session he'd had with Quanice.

Joshua insisted that Quanice take his regular breaks, but Joshua barely had time to use the toilet and drink more water and coffee.

He really hoped the shop's luck was turning around. But at any rate, Quanice said he already had some ideas. Joshua asked him to type them up and include any resources Quanice thought he should look at. Joshua would pay for his time.

Now that he thought of it, having a resource actively working for him was already a sign that things were shifting for the better.

With your magical hat back on, you can start looking at what's actually happening instead of just what you think should happen. Or wish could happen.

He'd still have to learn the marketing stuff himself eventually, but having guidance under his roof? That was a pretty big boon.

Looking out the window at the semi-industrial Foster Road, Joshua wondered how much longer it would be before the small pockets of shops, bars, and the occasional café or restaurant turned into long stretches of the same, the way his NE neighborhood was now pretty thoroughly gentrified. Of course, he was part of that process, he supposed. He was just a white guy from Oregon City. Northeast Portland had been a different—Blacker—world when he was born.

A lot of people were moving out this way now, some of them heading even further east, out to the neighborhoods that long-time locals called "the numbers."

The Mercado wasn't that far out, ensconced just west of 205, in the still-kind-of-working-class-for-the-moment neighborhood of Foster-Powell. It was comprised of a building with a market, a butcher, and a small café inside and a collection of food trucks actually owned by Latin American cooks and businesspeople on the outside. The Mercado was sure to be jammed on a sunny weekday evening.

Frater Louis said he would arrive early and try to snag a table in the little wine and beer garden situated on the outer edge of the building, skirting the food cart area. He'd already texted Legis his food order, he said, which prompted Joshua to do the same.

Apparently, the Gods had decreed today "educate Joshua day." He wasn't going to fight it anymore. The Universe wanted him to get his shit together, and then started throwing both major challenges and major help his way? He was going to pay attention.

Even if he felt a little stupid. The *should know better and wasted years and yadda yadda,* all that self-loathing self-talk.

He was sure the deprecation would surprise the people who bought into his dandy cock-of-the-walk persona, complete with the "I'm a capable magician" glamour. Hell, he'd even believed it himself, for awhile.

The bus *ssshhdd* to a stop in front of the bright Mercado courtyard. Sure enough, the tables beneath the long sun shelter were pretty full.

He walked past the multicolored food trucks toward the building on the back end of the property. Frater Louis waved a skinny arm his way. Legis sat across from him. Looked as though they already had food.

"Good timing!" Frater Louis said. "Legis just arrived with our orders."

"Hey, man. Good to see you. Grab a beer and sit," Legis said.

Joshua entered the small, inside bar area. A Japanese American man was behind the wooden bar, pulling pints and pouring wine. Joshua scanned the chalkboard, settling on a Willamette Pinot Gris. Cold white wine on a hot day sounded great, even though Legis would give him shit for not ordering beer.

It was just the way he showed love.

Wine in hand, he headed back to the table. Dazzled by the sun, he almost tripped. Damn. Yeah. He was still a little out of it from the night before.

"You okay?" Legis asked, as Joshua slid onto the bench.

"Just...things have been more than a little bit intense." He took a sip of wine. Crisp, clear, and cold, with just a hint of grapefruit at the finish. "Thanks so much for meeting me."

"Of course, brother," Frater Louis said.

"About that," Joshua said. "Can I come in sometime and talk about what all initiation requires?"

Legis set down his pint and shoved a plate of tacos Joshua's way. "You know I'll sponsor you, man. I've been waiting to for years."

Joshua felt the prick of tears and took another drink of wine. "Thanks, man. I had no idea."

"I try not to push my religion on other people," Legis said with a grin. "Eat your tacos, and drink your wine, asshole."

Joshua did. Carne asada, moist, with cabbage on top and radish on the side. There was also what looked like a very good summer veggie taco.

Once the men had made a dent in their food, Frater Louis wiped his mouth with a paper napkin and cleared his throat.

"You said you wanted to talk to us? About some magic? Legis told me about what happened with the servitor. What do you need to know?"

Joshua chewed and swallowed, then dabbed at his own mouth. "Well, I know more about them now than I did this morning. I remembered my employee is a Chaote and he gave me some information in between customers today."

"Well, chaos magicians are definitely the ones to ask," Legis commented, before shoving another half a taco in his maw. "They deal with servitors more than any other magic workers I know." The guy was so big, Joshua sometimes wondered how many calories he needed just to get through the day.

Joshua sipped at his wine, then cleared his throat, wishing he had some ice water. Gods, even under the awning structure, the sun was hot today.

"But we're going to need to come at this from as many

angles as possible," he said. "So I wondered if you two could figure out how to get a magical being to change allegiance? Is that even possible?"

Legis polished off his plate and glanced at his almost empty pint glass.

"Before we get into this, you owe me a beer for getting online for our food."

"Fair enough," Joshua said. "Frater Louis?"

"I'm good," the wiry man replied.

Joshua wiped his hands again and headed back into the little bar. He stood behind a person ordering three different kinds of beer, waiting to place his order for Legis's pint.

His phone buzzed. It was Brenda, asking if he could bring some more of the flying ointment to the meeting the coven had planned for the next evening.

He texted back a quick *Sure!* Then he thought for a moment and thumbed another message. *With Legis and Fra Louis. Want them at the meeting, too?* He paid for Legis's beer, and a second glass of wine and asked for three cups of iced water.

His phone buzzed again. *If they're available, that'd be great,* the text read.

He texted back a thumbs-up emoji and grabbed a tray.

The two men had finished their food in his absence and looked ready to talk. Joshua passed the drinks around, picked up his remaining taco, and said "Servitors? Changing allegiance? Oh, and Brenda wants to know if you two are available for a meeting tomorrow evening."

"I should be able to shuffle some things around," Legis said.

"And I don't have anything on for tomorrow night, although—" Frater Louis checked his wrist "—I do need to be at the lodge in an hour to start setting up for tonight's class."

Frater Louis took a long swallow of ice water, set the sweating cup down on the wood table, steepled his fingers, and began speaking.

"Servitors, in general, are designed by and powered by a magician's intention, will, and life energy. The magician, in almost all cases, is the only one with the proper key, so to speak, to make the servitor work."

Legis set his beer down and chimed in. "There are a few notable exceptions to that, like Fotamecus, the time-shifting servitor, who works for anyone who knows its sigil."

Joshua frowned, and drank more wine, trying to thread together a bunch of associations flying through his head. The second glass of wine had likely been bad idea. He set the glass down with a sigh and held up a hand.

"Wait a minute," he said. "Does using a sigil make a servitor like an angel, or a goetic demon or something? Do they act the same way? And how about golems?"

Frater Louis smiled. "Golems are servitors made of clay, so they are a pretty good example. The rabbi is the only one who knows the sacred word carved on the golem's head to give it life. A golem is linked only to the rabbi's will. Angels or demons, however, are their own creatures. They have a life outside their work with us."

Joshua sat back. Okay. This was making a strange sort of sense.

"So breaking a link between a servitor and its creator? How do you do that?" he asked.

"It's almost impossible," Legis replied, balling up his napkin.

"Well shit," Joshua replied. How the hell were they going to fight this arrogant toad of a man? He'd really thought

Selene had an in with the servitor. "Even if the servitor seems unhappy?"

"You can always trick the magician into giving the servitor a sock..." Legis quipped.

Joshua balled up his own napkin and threw it at the big man.

Frater Louis rapped on the table. "Legis said 'almost impossible'."

A tiny flicker of hope flared in Joshua's chest.

"You mean?"

"We'll work on it." Frater Legis rose from the table. "But I have to open up the lodge for tonight's class. You should start showing up, Joshua."

Joshua nodded. "I will. Once all of this is over."

Frater Louis and Legis both shook their heads.

"This stuff will never be over," Legis replied. "There's always going to be something. You, my man, just need to learn to commit."

Joshua nodded. He knew that. He did. And he was inching closer to it, bit by bit.

But for now? He was going to finish his glass of wine, enjoy the sun, and talk magic with his friend Legis, who still had half a pint left in front of him.

If he couldn't solve the world's problems, he could at least enjoy the moment, right?

That would have to be good enough for now.

25

SELENE

Selene was filled with an overwhelming sense of sorrow. No. Not sorrow. Grief. Heartrending, aching, grief.

Tabitha's spirit was being held captive. She had sounded so frightened and alone, and Selene truly had no idea how to help.

The blazing sun bouncing off the sidewalk and buildings just made everything feel worse. There was no softening of reality. No avoidance of the pain. Just the unrelenting brightness that left them once again feeling overexposed and wishing they were numb.

But they were going to work anyway. Because self-numbing was a thing of Selene's past. A seductive, watery grave.

Selene still held on to hope for the return of Tabitha's spirit, but had to admit there was no certainty that her parents could give her enough juice to survive. No guarantee that the coven's magic could reach Tabitha before her soul was completely drained away. And what happened to a person when someone else had siphoned off their soul?

There was no metaphysical treatise on that, as far as Selene knew.

Maybe that person just...ended. And for a spirit as bright and filled with creative spark as Tabitha? No. Selene couldn't abide that. It would not stand. They *had* to find some way to fix the damned situation.

Selene had also finally admitted that Janice's death had rocked them harder than they admitted at first. But even touching that thought felt more painful than Selene could bear.

The closest parking they found for the studio was four blocks away, so they were walking in the heat, long black summer skirt swirling around their Chuck Taylors, messenger bag with tablet and pencils inside slung across their chest. They hoped to find the wherewithal to do some more work for clients. Bills were coming due and there was wallowing to avoid. They also felt a need to look at the still life again. There was something in the painting that seemed significant in the face of recent events, but Selene wasn't sure what, yet.

All they were certain of today was that their body felt leaden and their heart was sore.

Even the jangle from the stack of bangles on their right wrist and their favorite tuberose essential oil perfume weren't lightening their mood. Selene had hoped they might. A for effort, C for execution.

In that moment, Selene wished they still smoked cigarettes.

Getting yanked back into their body the night before had jostled their soul in a way that only seemed to highlight all their weaknesses. The places they kept patching over, because being a tall, non-binary femme trying to make their way in the world was difficult and dangerous enough that they just had to pretend everything was Goddess-damned just okay.

And it wasn't. It never was, and maybe it never would be. And the patches weren't as strong as they had thought. But here they were, a person with a great coven who genuinely cared about them, and work that *did* pay the bills, actually, and only seemed to be increasing if the good word of mouth continued. It was all true. That which seemed bad and that which seemed good.

Plus, there was the river, right? Selene sniffed and wiped their nose, deciding to walk a few blocks down a deserted, industrial side street toward the water. They just wanted a moment alone to stare at the watery ribbon of light that bordered the slice of neighborhood east of MLK.

Selene turned, walking toward the tangle of freeway to get a better view of the river. Getting to the actual esplanade was too tricky on this stretch. Too much highway and major streets. But a closer look, Selene could manage.

They walked in the temporary shade thrown by the tall self-storage building, next to the location where the Portland Night Market was held. They decided to stop there for a moment. Give themselves some respite from the sun.

The sound of the highway was loud here, but they didn't mind. Loving nature, Selene was also an urban creature. Humans had built the city, after all. It was one of the things their type of animal did.

Selene stared and breathed, lifting their hair off their neck, trying to get some air onto damp skin. The view of the water and the breathing calmed them a little, but the grief remained.

Selene breathed into their center and felt their feet, solid on the sidewalk in their canvas high-tops. They reached with their energy, attention, and imagination, from where they stood, past the freeway overpasses and the straight line of I-5. The energy of distant cars rushing by shook the edges of their aura, even here, on this semi-deserted, industrial street.

And then there was the cool flowing of water. The top layer was warmed by the dappling sun. Selene breathed more deeply, and sank down a layer.

The water was cool there. Darker. They let the sense of liquid bathe them. Soothe them like the light of the moon did.

Wash away some of the hard encrustations that grief and anger had left marked on their spirit from that childhood where everything had tried to crush what was real inside them. To batter them down and rebuild them into something more normal than they could ever be.

Selene closed their eyes and simply *felt* for a while, surrounded by the sense of water.

It was nice to feel good.

Their awareness began pinging the edges of their aura. They needed to come back. Be present. Actually finish the short walk to the studio and get to work.

Designs weren't going to draw themselves.

They turned back toward MLK. From there, they would turn right and head south toward Morrison and the studio. Still lost in the feel of water, Selene didn't even mind too much when they had to step back into the brightness of midday.

A person stepped out from a doorway, face in shadow. Selene moved to skirt around them, pasting on one of those fake, looking-harmless-for-a-stranger half smiles. The person stepped into Selene's path, blocking the way.

Selene stood taller and replaced the smile with a scowl.

"Excuse me, please." They made their voice strong,

though it was always a gamble in these situations. Pitch the voice high, they might see Selene as less of a threat. Pitch it low, they might obey and let them pass. But that scenario could easily reverse itself. Just such a gamble had gotten Selene's left radius bone cracked and broken out two teeth that had to be replaced with money Selene just didn't have. They were still paying off the debt.

The person didn't move. Selene was close enough now to see their face. It looked familiar. They scrambled through the files in their tired brain, searching for a match. Nope. Couldn't place the person.

The person—who looked like a cis man—wore black pants and a white shirt with a teal pocket square tucked neatly in front.

His ice-blue eyes stared at Selene. The hairs on Selene's arms rose. So did the small hairs at the nape of their neck. That sense of something walking over their grave was back. Here.

Under the Goddess-damned bright summer sun.

26

JOSHUA

Back on the bus after his second glass of wine, Joshua was heading home. He'd have to transfer to a second bus in order to head to NE Portland, but he didn't mind much. The bus was always interesting, and if not, he had podcasts to listen to and books to read.

Today, he looked out the window at the light industrial warehouses giving way to houses, restaurants, and the new condo complexes that were springing up all over the city in an attempt to arrest the housing crisis. He was still thinking about magic, and servitors, and possible manipulative cult leaders.

Magical practice was supposed to tune people into the cosmos and help them work toward liberation. To use magic to manipulate people was just evil, in Joshua's book.

He had almost walked over to the temple for the class Frater Louis was leading, but that second glass of wine dissuaded him. He wouldn't be able to focus properly on whatever the topic was. He should just get himself home. Maybe do some study on his own. It wasn't as if his house didn't have a tidy little occult library that he hadn't looked at in months.

The bus wound its way north, en route to turn on to Hawthorne and then head across the river to downtown. The closer they got to Hawthorne, the more antsy Joshua began to feel. That was strange. It almost felt as if someone had put hotfoot powder in his shoes. He wanted nothing more than to leap off the bus and run.

Calm down, he told himself, and looked around. Everyone else on the bus seemed calm, except for one possibly houseless man having an agitated conversation with himself. The others on the bus read, scrolled their phones, or talked with one another.

Definitely just him. He began to itch.

The bus turned and trundled two blocks down Hawthorne. Four blocks down, he couldn't stand it anymore and pulled the cord. The bus *ssshhed* to a stop. Joshua grabbed his purse, smacked the back doors with his hands, and tumbled out onto the sidewalk.

He looked around, bewildered. Damn. The wine shouldn't have affected him this way. Something tugged at his solar plexus, as if there was a cord attached there, and someone was pulling on it.

Joshua began walking toward The Road Home. The tension eased. He immediately felt better. No more itching. No more tugging. Just the certainty that yes, he was heading the right direction.

As he approached the orange door, he felt it again, that sense of unease. The fairy lights still lit the branches in the front windows, but the rest of the shop was dark. Clearly closed. Just the way he and Quanice had left it. So why...?

He fumbled his keys from his pocket, unlocked the door, and stepped inside. Along with the regular incense and oil smells was the pungent scent of shorted-out electrical. That didn't make any sense. The new alarm system he'd ordered hadn't been installed yet, and if the breakers had blown, the fairy lights would be out.

Joshua hit the switches near the front, turning on the burbling fountain and the rest of the shop lights. At first glance, nothing seemed out of place, and the shop was quiet.

But everything still felt wrong.

He made his way between the fanciful birch trees, underneath the flying fairies, past the children's books and toys, the anointing oils, and on toward the more serious "adult" sections, including talismans, jewelry, and magical tools.

The display cases seemed untouched. He looked toward the curtain leading to the back, and all his inner alarms went off. He pushed through the burgundy velvet and looked down the short hallway that led to the WC and storage room. The door leading out to the garbage cans was slightly ajar. As Joshua walked closer, he saw that the doorjamb was splintered.

"What the—?"

But they hadn't taken anything from the shop. At least it didn't look like it.

He trailed his hand along the wall, trying to think through the mild wine haze. And more importantly, trying to *sense*.

The storeroom.

The door knob was slick, which was weird. It left an oily residue on Joshua's hand. He slammed the door open, eyes raking the small table where they packed items for shipping, and the shelves that flanked the room.

There was a hole in the shelf to the right.

The flying ointment was gone.

Joshua cursed. He couldn't imagine what would make someone drop off the box of ointment in the first place, let alone break into a shop to steal it back.

"Of course." The thought hit him so hard he might as well have smacked a palm to his forehead. "The cops. The cops have a jar of the ointment. Can't leave more evidence strewn around town."

Joshua wondered how widely distributed the Alchemist's wares had been. And was he using it on his students?

He must be, right?

All of this was still just speculation. A customer here and there. Fliers. Comments.

And people dying.

His face popped with sweat and his mouth filled with spit. His hands. The damn spiked flying ointment. The ozone smell was magic.

Joshua cursed and ran for the shop toilet. Slamming his left hand against the cold water faucet, he plunged his right hand under the water. Soap. He needed soap. Holding his hand beneath the soap dispenser, he smacked his other hand against it, disgorging a glob of pale goo which he smushed around his palm. Smush. Rinse. Glob. Smush. Rinse. Glob.

He finally trusted that enough of the toxic substance had rinsed down the drain to rub his hands together, giving his skin a more thorough wash. Sweat still ran down his face. He blinked to keep it from his eyes.

Who the hell were these people? And what did they want?

Joshua stopped washing his hands.

"Shit." Turning the water off, he grabbed paper towels and scrubbed at his skin some more.

No shortness of breath, but he still needed medical attention.

Joshua dug out his phone. But who to call? He pulled up his car service app first; there was no time to wait for a friend to come from wherever they were to fetch him.

Joshua's mouth filled with spit and his stomach roiled. He blinked and tried to focus on his phone. The car was en route. Good. No heart palpitations yet. Also good.

With clumsy thumbs, Joshua tried to text Quanice before giving up and using voice to text. *Emergency. Shop broken into. Heading to urgent care. You free to come by shop? Call a locksmith? Back door.*

?!?! Urgent care? was the reply. Then a pause.

Then, *I'll get there ASAP. Looking up locksmiths now.*

Thanks. Joshua texted back. *And don't touch the storeroom door. It's poisoned.*

?!?!

Grabbing a paper towel so he wouldn't have to touch the car door once it arrived, he pushed out the broken back door and shouldered it as shut as it would go. No time to secure it further. No time to reset any magical wards.

He'd have to clear the space and do that, later. For now he had to get to urgent care before things got any worse.

27

SELENE

"Do I know you?" Selene asked.

The man clucked his tongue, making small *tsking* noises.

"I'm so disappointed in you, Selene. To have forgotten me so quickly? I most certainly have remembered you."

Selene's stomach lurched. The edges of their skin flashed hot, cold, hot, cold, hot.

Nononono. Not now.

Selene willed breath into their lungs. They willed the arms they'd wrapped around their torso to unfurl, and their hands to unclench. They willed their feet to connect with earth.

Moon Mother, if you are here, help me now.

Selene took in a deep breath and remembered that they were a witch. With a coven. And a career. And a life worth living.

"Who are you?"

He smiled. A sick, saccharine, patronizing smile.

Selene remembered. That night in the club. One year before.

"You bastard," they spit out. "You tried to *rape* me."

The man made that sickening *tsk tsk* sound again.

"Now, now. That isn't how I remembered it. I bought you a drink. We danced. We went to the bathroom to get to know each other better. Things followed from there."

He had roofied Selene's drink in the club that night. Then followed Selene toward the toilets and grabbed them in the dark hallway just as Selene's head started to spin from the drugs. They remembered it. The way their vision fuzzed and refocused. Fuzzed and refocused. He had pressed his mouth against theirs. His lips were thin. Hard and moist. Selene could feel his teeth behind the flesh.

He had tasted like whiskey and ash. Selene hadn't been able to drink whiskey since.

Tabitha happened to be coming out of the women's toilets right then and went to grab her girlfriend of the moment. The two of them intervened before anything worse happened and got Selene safely home to bed. The room had revolved around Selene for what felt like hours as Tabitha tried to get them to sip some water and stroked their hair.

Selene's skin had flashed hot and cold, body waiting to disgorge the contents of their stomach. They had vomited three times that night. *Damn it.*

The man's eyes swept across her face with some twisted version of fond affection. "You're still so beautiful. The most beautiful creature I've seen in quite a while." Then his mouth hardened and his pupils dilated. "And I bet you have a very sweet ass."

"Get away from me." Selene was shaking now, breath coming fast. They weren't sure if it was from fear or anger. Their fingers twitched, wishing for a spell bag.

Wishing for their athamé, to blast this fool with a stream of blue magic fire.

They had nothing but themselves.

Selene stepped off the sidewalk and ran, darting across the deserted street, heading east, toward traffic and people. Their sneakers smacked the sidewalk opposite, messenger bag bouncing against their right hip.

The man chased after, grabbing the bag, jerking Selene back and slamming them up against a wall. Selene's cheek ground against the faded wood siding. His hand was on their ass, squeezing muscle, clutching at their skirt.

"Want to show it to me? Do you? I'll make it good for you. I promise. I can show you things...."

Selene raised a foot and stomped back, connecting with his insole. He yelped, hands losing their grip for just a second.

Goddess help me.

Selene flung themself backward, slamming their hand low, smacking their fist and that stack of metal bracelets where they thought his crotch might be. Connected. Yielding softness.

"Fuck!" he yelled, grabbing their arm again. "You bitch!"

The man dragged at them, still hunched in half, trying to protect his crotch. Selene pulled.

"Hey! Leave her alone!" A voice. Feet running. Selene yanked their arm away just as the man let go.

He ran, lumbering and hitching down the street.

Selene bent over, panting, then fell to the curb and vomited into the street.

Hands on their back, gentle ones this time.

"Hey. Hey. Are you all right? Lady?"

Selene sat down on the sidewalk and wiped their mouth.

"Do you want some water?" A metal water flask, offered at eye level.

Selene looked up, blinking. A man. Brown skin. Work boots.

Selene nodded and he unscrewed the cap. Selene took some water, swished, and spit into the gutter. Then drank.

"Sorry about that; you might want to wash it before drinking out of it again," they said.

The man crouched next to them and took the bottle back. "Doesn't matter. I was just on a lunch break and saw him.... Do you want me to call the police?"

He looked skeptical. Whether it was because he had just realized Selene might not be a lady, or that he was a brown-skinned man, Selene didn't know.

Selene shook their head. "No. Thank you. Thank you so much for saving me. I was trying to fight him but..."

"Pendejo. Men like that are worse than useless."

Selene's cheeks were wet. When had they started crying?

"Can I help you up? Call someone? Get you somewhere?"

Selene looked at him. So earnest. Solid. Kind.

"Can you walk me to my car?"

"You okay to drive? I mean, you sure you don't want to call someone? I'd take you, but my boss..."

"No. No. Thanks. You're right though. I probably shouldn't drive. I rent studio space just a block away. Can you walk me there?"

He nodded and offered Selene a hand. Goddess, their body was really messed up. This week had gone from bad to worse.

"You're an artist, huh? I'd like to see what you paint sometime. I used to paint, too, a long time ago."

"You're welcome to visit the studio anytime.... What's your name?"

"Jorge."

"Jorge. Nice to meet you. My name is Selene."

Child of the Moon Goddess. And a freaking mess.

They walked in silence for the remaining couple of blocks.

"Here we are," Selene said, once they were in front of the two-story ancient warehouse, now painted a cheery light blue. "Thank you so much for helping me."

Selene's voice sounded hollow to themself, but they hoped Jorge heard the sincerity all the same.

He gave a slight bow and turned around, walking back to wherever it was he'd been headed. Maybe he still had enough time left on his break to get some lunch.

As they turned, the pale blue paint layered on the chipped and gouged wood surrounding the front windows triggered another memory. Something someone had said. Joshua.

Blue. Those colors. The man. White. Black. Teal.

Was that drugging rapist asshole the Alchemist?

The hairs stood up on Selene's arms again, and the nape of their neck prickled.

Well. Selene's mouth tightened. They'd just become an angry bitch.

"You messed with the wrong enby, asshole. I've got a coven, and we're going to take you down."

28

JOSHUA

Joshua's phone rang while he was still in urgent care. Brenda told him to come over if he could. Selene had been attacked. Not just attacked. Assaulted.

He told her that he'd been poisoned, like Lucy. And he'd be there as soon as he could.

Good Gods, could the day get any worse?

Declaring him okay, the doctor finally released Joshua, explaining that the clinic would be calling both Poison Control and the police, and would be in touch. She also made him promise to come back if any symptoms returned.

When the car dropped him at Brenda's house, Selene wasn't there.

Joshua almost blew a gasket when Tobias and Raquel told him they'd let Selene go home alone. No fucking way would he leave a person he loved after they'd been assaulted.

"Are you people *crazy*?" he had yelled. Brenda and Raquel had told him what they knew, and Tobias filled in more after he arrived.

"Selene really wanted to be alone. I did my best, man. But they insisted."

Brenda had put a hand on his shoulder. "Selene is an empath. Being around strong emotions right now would be too much for them. It doesn't matter what we want. We've been through this before. We have to honor Selene's wishes."

Joshua shook Brenda's hand off. "I don't know what sort of agreements you all have with each other. All I know is, if a friend of mine had been assaulted, I would be there. Holding onto them. Telling them I cared. And the fact that it looks like it might have been the fucking *Alchemist*? Come. On!"

He'd slammed out of the house at that point, called Legis to come get him, and raced to Selene's building.

Now he stood outside an old, three-story white Victorian with black trim and a gorgeous wraparound porch, wondering if he was a fool.

Or if he should have brought flowers. Or tea. Or wine. Reality was, he was still shaky from the poisoning and in no condition to do anything other than stand and stare. He wasn't even sure if he could make it up the stairs.

Or if he should have even come.

Joshua sighed. Well, he was here now. Legis had asked if he wanted him to wait around, just in case, but Joshua had said no. If Selene didn't want him here, he'd make his own way home.

Legis had looked dubious, but just said "Call me, man," put his car in gear and driven off.

Joshua walked up the peeling white front steps, toward the glossy black door. It had a leaded glass window inserted in the top half. He could make out a white-painted staircase heading up, and the straight shot of a long hallway heading back.

There were five buzzers to the right side of the door. The bottom one just had an image. A crescent moon.

Selene.

He buzzed, and stood, planting his feet in their navy blue wingtips on the grand, peeling porch.

Nothing.

He buzzed again.

A crackling sound. "Yes?"

"Selene. It's Joshua. I know you don't want to see anyone...but I really want to see *you*." He paused. Dead air greeted him. Not even the sound of breathing.

"Selene? May I see you?"

Another pause. Then a buzz and a click. Joshua grabbed the door latch and pushed his way in. Then, taking it slowly, he started to climb.

When he reached the top, Selene was waiting there, dressed in the most glorious black floor-length robe with peonies skirting the bottom third and climbing up the right side.

They wore no makeup, and Joshua was startled by the fineness of their face. The slightly square jaw. The perfectly arched eyebrows, a little thinner than usual. The high cheekbones, the right one scraped red, as though someone had taken sandpaper to the ghostly skin. Joshua flushed with anger. How could someone have done this?

Selene's lips were pale, almost disappearing in their face. Joshua wanted nothing more than to kiss them.

Selene looked tired, eyes wary.

"What are you doing here?" they asked.

"I had to see you. I heard...and I had to see you. Selene. You shouldn't be alone."

Joshua stood on the tiny attic landing, at the top of the steep attic stairs, and waited. He felt his breath rasping in and out of his chest from the climb.

Selene, pale as the moon, bare-faced, just looked at him. Looked at his face. Joshua felt as if no one had ever looked at him like that.

No one had ever seen him. Not really. Not since Jessie had been killed.

"Come in," Selene said, and took a step back. Joshua followed, stepping into a tiny jewel box filled with wonders. A painting eave, with a drop cloth on the floor and jars of brushes. Statuary. Art on the walls. Small, plush rugs scattered here and there on dark plank floors. A high bed, dressed in burgundy and gold.

"Can I get you tea?" Selene asked, then cleared their throat. "Wine? You look like you're in pretty bad shape yourself."

Joshua realized he was standing stock still, barely inside the entryway, just staring.

"Um. Tea would be great. Thank you." No wine. His body still felt burned with toxins.

"Feel free to have a seat."

He felt so awkward. As if he were intruding. He followed Selene to the tiny kitchen tucked into the eaves. Selene turned with efficiency. Filling the electric kettle. Setting out cups. Opening canisters and sniffing. Cradling a green ceramic pot in long, pale fingers as they brought it down from a top shelf.

The dance of tea. Elegant. The way Selene was.

"Do you want to talk about it?" he finally asked.

The water rumbled, just below boil. Selene turned and flicked it off.

"Not really. Not now."

The way Selene had stared at him on the landing, as if they truly saw him? Well, they wouldn't even look at Joshua now.

He stepped into the kitchen. Not sure if it was the right thing.

"Hey," he said, then put his hands on Selene's shoulders. Felt the long muscles of their upper arms. Selene flinched and looked down, dark hair curtaining their face. He let go.

"Selene? Can you look at me? Will you?"

He heard the sharp intake of air, then the slower exhalation. A soft swallow.

And Selene raised their head. Their eyes held such pain, Joshua's knees almost buckled. But they held their dark eyes steady on his own. Showing him everything. Almost too much. He did not look away.

"Selene. I..." What were the words? *Take a risk.* "May I hold you?"

That pause again. So many pauses. Then a nod. A ripple of dark hair.

Joshua slid his arms around Selene, one arm cradling their shoulders, the other slipping around their slender waist. He drew them to his chest, where, because they were barefoot, their head tucked just so beneath his chin.

They held themself so stiff, it almost felt as if Joshua were holding glass.

He began to slowly sway, rocking Selene's body with his own.

"You're safe now. Thank the Gods, you're safe. And people love you. And you're beautiful." The words just kept coming. "And they don't want to be too much for you, they're just trying to tell you...how much they care about you. That they want you here. And not to run away. And..."

Joshua felt a shuddering inhalation against his chest. An attempt to clear a throat thick with incipient tears.

"I'm not sure I can trust you..." they said.

Joshua pulled away just enough to look down at their beautiful face, then drew Selene close again, feeling the slight relaxation of their body against his.

"I know," he said. "But maybe we can learn together."

They stood in Selene's pocket kitchen, tea forgotten, just breathing together. Breathing and rocking, auras slowly softening, opening, blending.

After a while—Joshua wasn't certain how long—they moved to a small loveseat, still nestled against one another.

Selene finally broke the silence, barely, with a muffled murmur into his shirtfront.

"It's been a long time."

"Since what?" he whispered into their hair, inhaling the tuberose scent of them.

"This."

And they tilted their beautiful naked face upward.

Joshua held Selene's gaze with his own, just for a moment. And then, breath by breath, millimeter by millimeter, their two faces drew closer.

And they kissed.

29

SELENE

Goddess, Selene was tired. Sore, too. They forced themself up. Out of bed. Make some tea. Eat a piece of toast with a smear of peanut butter. Crawl into the tub. Again.

After Tobias had reluctantly dropped Selene off the night before, the first thing they did was strip off all their clothes and climb into the tub, heat be damned.

They needed the comfort of it. And their bruised knees and abraded face did, too.

And they needed to scrub that bastard's hands off of their body. Apparently they weren't done with that, yet.

Selene ran the rough washcloth over their lips for what must have been the hundredth time, trying to scrape away his sick perversion of a kiss.

After Joshua had left last night, it was all Selene could do to crawl up into bed. They had really wanted to do magic, but sleep claimed their body and mind before the thought was even half-formed.

So here they were, soaking in tepid water in the huge clawfoot tub in a bathroom that had been the major selling point when Selene decided to rent this place three years ago. The apartment had always been just slightly beyond their budget, but the light through the windows, and this tub, made it worthwhile.

The coven was freaking out. Selene didn't blame them. They would be, too. But Selene really didn't want the fussing, though they were grateful they hadn't needed to drive themself home from the studio after the assault.

They had called Brenda, who had called Tobias, who had come picked Selene up. The coven always came through.

They were grateful. But then they really just needed to be home. Alone. Maybe to lick their wounds? Selene shook their head. Maybe. They didn't know. All they knew was they had needed to be home and to not have to explain anything. They were still too raw to field everyone's concern, and anger, and fear. Selene didn't have the wherewithal right now to shield themself from it. Not even from coven members who knew about shielding and boundaries and keeping their own emotional states to themselves. When someone you loved was hurt, sometimes your boundaries came down.

Even more than the fussing and worry, Selene couldn't bear the pain and love they knew would be in their coven mates' eyes. That just might break Selene. And Selene needed to feel strong.

"Enough." Selene's fingers were pruning again, just as they had last night. They pulled the drain plug and stood to dry off with a fluffy, wine-colored towel as the water gurgled down into the pipes in a clockwise spiral. Stepping out of the tub, they dried their feet with care, slathered on a layer of lotion, and slipped back into their peony-embroidered, floor-length robe.

They paused at the vanity for a moment, and dabbed some tuberose oil in the crook of each elbow, behind each ear, and in the hollow between their collarbones.

Selene loved every person in Arrow and Crescent but couldn't afford to be around dropped boundaries right now. Besides, Selene had told Tobias everything they knew as he drove them home the night before. Once was enough. They couldn't go through it again. He could tell everyone what had happened.

All Selene wanted were the wards and protections of their home space, away from the clamor of other people's hearts.

They left the bathroom and wandered barefooted through the little paint box apartment, across the scarred wood floors and jewel-like rugs. The queen size bed Selene had found second hand sat in the far corner. It had a dark walnut slatted headboard and was draped with a comforter of burgundy and gold. The bed was still appealing, but Selene forced themself past it.

The jutting dormer area that housed their ersatz home studio was awash with brightness. The windows looked out onto a towering fir tree that Selene loved. No painting this morning. They just didn't have it in them. Not yet. Perhaps this afternoon.

What they needed now was magic.

Magic that had nothing to do with chasing down rapist magicians trying to control and manipulate other people for their own ends.

Magic that didn't have anything to do with anyone except Selene, and Selene's heart, and Selene's mind.

Selene needed the moon.

And they needed to not let that asshole take magic away from them. He had already cheated them of their usual full moon rite this month by sending Tabitha to the hospital.

Morning wasn't Selene's usual time, but they needed the comfort and solidity of ritual. Selene needed communion.

So, hair still damp from trailing in the bath water, they padded past the seating area toward the chest filled with magical herbs and accouterment.

Selene crouched, knees complaining, next to the wooden cedar chest. Damn. They must have hit the concrete hard. Opening the lid, they pulled out a shallow scrying bowl wrapped in a deep purple cloth. A container of kosher salt. Two fresh beeswax tapers. Incense? No. They didn't need it.

Selene carefully laid out their ritual objects on the low, round wood table set between two black-cloth-covered easy chairs and Selene's recent thrift store find of a dark navy velvet loveseat.

They unwrapped the bowl first, flicking the purple cloth open on the table. It would serve as an altar cloth. They centered the bowl, a hand-thrown ceramic piece glazed in a swirl of blacks, purples, blues, and a brown as deep as earth. Made by one of the students at school. Selene had bought it at the yearly winter fair.

Maybe it would have been better to wait for full dark, but Selene was tired and needed the comfort of connection right now. They needed to touch the knowledge that, no matter what happened to them, they were still a child of the moon.

Besides, the moon was always present, whether Selene could see it or not. And they did catch its face during daylight sometimes. That was a reminder, too.

Maybe Selene could learn to be seen even under harsh light.

They just didn't know if they could, even though it had felt good to be with Joshua last night. To just sit and breathe, head cradled on his shoulder. After a while, Selene had even forgotten to be anxious.

And that kiss... It had been sweet. Nice. His lips were warm and full, nothing like the Alchemist's mouth. Selene shuddered, and flicked their fingers as if to banish the thought of the man. Joshua was a much better memory.

And Selene carried the image of his face close. A talisman against things in the world that felt bad.

Maybe he was one more person who saw Selene for what they actually were.

Rising again, Selene wandered through the little attic apartment, closing heavy drapes, dropping the light level more toward a winter dusk than summer morning.

Selene made the circuit to their tiny kitchen and filled a pitcher with clear water.

Back at the seating area, they poured the water into the scrying bowl and set the pitcher aside. They lit the candles, then rose and untied their robe. They would greet their Goddess naked. Clean.

To Her, they would risk being exposed. Always.

Tears rolled down Selene's face as they raised their arms in supplication.

"Mother Moon. Sister Moon. Sibling Moon. Cousin Moon. Brother Moon. You who bear so many names offered by so many people. Hear me. See me. Be with me. I bear one of your many names. I too, like you, am neither male nor female. I choose you, just as you chose me. I call you Mother, though I know you are much more than that. I name you Moon because of the way light reflects through and around you, bringing beauty from the velvet dark."

Selene paused, adjusting their weight on the balls of their feet. Took another breath.

"Help me to see my face and know myself. Guide me on the luminous paths of power. Give me insight…" Their voice broke then, and their chest caved, just a little, before Selene caught themself and stood upright again. Another breath. Then a deeper one. Inhale. Exhale.

"Give me insight into what I need to help those in need. Danger walks our city. It…it has violated me…."

Re-center, Selene. Keep breathing. This was harder than Selene thought it would be. Maybe the coven was right. They should have been around friends after the attack. Or maybe they should have just crawled back into bed.

Selene knelt in front of the altar, knees cushioned by the soft floor rug, and inhaled deeply.

"Mother Moon, show me your face. Help me to walk the paths of darkness."

Selene was repeating themselves, but right now? It was the only prayer they knew.

"Mother Moon…"

Selene gazed into the dark reflecting bowl, saw the flicker of candle flames like sparks deep in the water.

Saw their own face. Half in darkness. Half in light. Never fully illuminated. Slipping through the shadows. Revealing only what they chose.

They knew that already. Was it just a confirmation?

Selene breathed across the water, ripples shattering the image until the water was still again.

All they could see now were the tiny, flickering candle flames.

They blinked. Refocused their eyes, and then softened their gaze again, breathing slowly.

The bowl filled with the image of the full moon. Just like

in the painting Selene was working on. Out from the depths of the water, the moon called all creatures to rise.

A slight pressure banded Selene's forehead, as if someone's hands were pressing there. As they stared into the image of the moon, a voice rang, clear and strong.

:Those who walk the pathways of darkness see into the night of other souls. Those who live in two worlds travel well. Seek the hidden pathway. See the truth.:

The image of the moon faded from the water. Selene exhaled, long and slow.

They'd been given a message.

They just had no idea what it meant.

30

JOSHUA

Joshua was on his usual route from the bus stop to The Road Home, except this morning, he was headed to the Inner Eye first. He needed to confer with Brenda, and to buy a small piece of magic.

The memory of Selene, head resting on his shoulder, wouldn't leave Joshua. He felt a sense of awe and affection, and a deep wish to protect them at all costs. The combination of power and vulnerability were so potent in Selene, and he wasn't certain they were aware of it.

He had loved Jessie, and wanted to protect her—and couldn't, in the end—but their relationship had been more like a coming home, not as if together, they just might set the world aflame.

He'd also had crushes before, even loved other people. But after Jessie died, it was always clear that he was a free agent and was never going to go that deep with anyone again.

But he might just want to go there with Selene.

As he walked to Brenda's shop, he pondered that Moon card. Things crawling up from the subconscious, toward the light. Well, Selene themself was the moon. It was right there, encoded in their name. Joshua couldn't think about it too much right now, but he also felt pretty damned determined to do what he could to help Selene.

And one thing he could do was to buy Selene a moonstone. He had no idea why, not yet, he just knew he'd awakened that morning with the idea in his head. His subconscious must be working overtime.

He really should have been at the shop with Quanice, clearing the space and resetting the wards. But that would have to wait. He'd spoken with Quanice this morning and told him they weren't opening the store today, but to please come in around one.

Joshua couldn't really afford to not open on a regular work day, what with Faery Fest cancelled and all, but he frankly still felt a little wobbly, and the magic necessary to get the shop back into some sort of metaphysical order was around all he had the energy for. He couldn't deal with customers too.

A throat cleared from a shadowed doorway. Joshua turned. White shirt. Black trousers. Peacock-teal silk necktie.

The Alchemist.

Not thinking, Joshua whirled, and threw a punch at the man's face. The Alchemist stepped to one side and laughed. Joshua barely caught himself before crashing into the door frame.

Damn it. Still weak.

"Attacking a man at his own doorstep? That's unsporting of you."

"You live here?"

"For now. It makes it easier to keep a watch on you and that charming witch Brenda. Who *should* be your competition, if you were actually any sort of a magician. Or a man."

"At least I know where to send the police now," Joshua remarked, getting his temper under control.

That laugh again. Like nails on a chalkboard.

"You can't prove anything," the Alchemist said. "And you barely have any magic. That much is clear. No one in this city has much, do they? I'm sorely disappointed."

Who *was* this jerk? He was practically a cartoon character.

"You assaulted someone, asshole. You think we can't prove that? And how many people have you poisoned so far?"

The Alchemist just smirked.

Joshua couldn't let his temper get the better of him. *Harness that life force*, he told himself. *Invoke your will.*

Despite the warm morning, he suddenly felt cool. Calm.

"Did you bust into my shop?" he asked.

The man flicked his fingers as if to bat away a fly.

"Your shop was broken into?" he asked, the face of innocence. His mouth hardened then. "You think I have no followers to work my will? What do you think those students of mine are for? It isn't for their innate alchemical ability."

The longer Joshua stood on the sidewalk, the less things made sense. Oh, the Alchemist was some sort of megalomaniac, that was clear. But his motivations were still opaque.

"What do you want with Selene?" Joshua finally asked, forcing the words from his lips. It was a question he didn't want to ask. Shouldn't ask. But it was also the only question that mattered to him.

A real smile skirted across the Alchemist's face. He looked toward the sky, then trained his ice-blue eyes back on Joshua.

"Ah. Selene. You're in love with them, too. I can't blame

you. I sent them a little present today, to let them know how special they are." He looked at his watch. "They should be getting it sometime in the next hour or so. Selene is rare and beautiful thing, which I don't think a man like you can fully comprehend."

He tapped a finger against his thin lips, then smiled again.

"Selene is the perfect alchemical creature," he said. "That's why I never let them go."

Blood roared through Joshua's head. He swung. Cartilage cracked. Blood gushed down the Alchemist's face.

The man doubled, hands over his face.

"You bastard!" he shrieked.

"Selene isn't a *creature*, you sick fuck. Leave them alone," Joshua replied. "Leave all of us alone."

The Alchemist scrabbled in his pants pocket for a handkerchief.

Joshua turned and walked toward the Inner Eye. He hoped Brenda had some ice for his knuckles and the right moonstone for Selene. And he really needed to sit down for a while. And contact Selene. Tell them he'd seen the Alchemist and that the asshole said he'd sent them a present.

At any rate, he'd take today as proof that sometimes the best magic worked directly on the earth plane, with whatever tools you had.

31

SELENE

After their ritual, Selene decided that crawling back into bed was not an option. So they were at the studio again, makeup covering their scraped cheek, listening to the chip of chisel on stone from the back room downstairs, and breathing in the familiar smells of graphite and paint.

They could have worked anywhere today, just designing on their tablet. But they had some animal need to get back to the studio and reclaim their space, especially after Joshua had texted to warn them the asshole was out there, stalking too close to coven home territory.

If Selene had learned one thing in all of their years as someone living just outside the realms of normalcy, it was that you couldn't cede your space to the assholes.

Assholes already owned the rest of the world, so if you did that, you ended up with nothing.

Selene sipped at the heavy purple mug filled with coffee. They needed to focus, being behind now on three client projects, plus the one for Lucy, who at least would be forgiving about it.

There had just been too much going on. Selene knew

that a witch should always be able to re-center and return to their focus, but lately? The overwhelming factor was just too much.

But they needed to try anyway.

As they drank, Selene flipped through some of the images they'd saved on their tablet for project number one. It was a book cover design for a small publisher. Their first. If they did well on this one, there would be more work to come. And Selene needed that. They flipped through images of shadowy streets, dark rivers, and a series of different poses from a lovely, thin, white woman with long dark hair. The model that was supposed to represent the protagonist.

Selene was learning a lot. The one cover design class at school had taught them the basics, but working to the specifications of a publisher was another matter entirely.

But today? Interesting as the work was? Focusing was still hard.

Selene was also going to have to meet with Arrow and Crescent. They knew the coven was still freaking out about the attack, and everything else, but Selene still felt so fragile about it all.

Including the visit from Joshua. That had been completely unexpected. And really nice, despite the fact that at one point, Selene had started crying on his shoulder. And the fact that Selene still wasn't sure how they felt about letting someone new in that close.

But perhaps they could take a breath and give it time.

Plus, there was still a cryptic message to decipher, and when was Selene going to have the mental and emotional space for that? They wished the Powers were less circumspect sometimes.

Tapping their stylus on the edge of the tablet, Selene

sighed. What they should really do was call their old therapist. See if he had an opening. A mid-40s trans man, Derrick was someone Selene could trust to at least have a chance of understanding what they were going through.

But money was still tight, and...

And you were just assaulted and really need help, Selene. Don't be stupid about this.

That was the voice of Selene's inner Brenda and Raquel. Somewhere in their coven training, the voices of the two women had blended into that of one wise advisor, who often showed up just to kick Selene's ass.

Okay. I'll call Derrick.

But for now, Selene really just needed to get some work done. Both to pay their rent, and for their mental and emotional well-being.

Selene needed to know there was one area of their life where they still had some measure of control.

There was a rap on the huge casement of the open doorway. Randy, a sculptor who worked the storefront shop stood there, holding a vase of red roses.

"Hey, Selene? Someone dropped this for you around thirty minutes ago. I just haven't had time to bring them up."

"Oh!" Selene swiveled off their stool and stalked across the broad plank floors, holding out their hands. "Thanks for bringing them up! Next time, feel free to text me."

"No problem. I needed a break, anyway." Randy transferred the vase over. It was heavy. "See you."

He clomped back down the stairs.

Selene sniffed at the blooms. Not much of interest there. Like so many hothouse flowers, these were grown for looks, not fragrance. They set the vase on their worktable and pulled the card out of the tiny envelope with a smile. Joshua really was sweet. Selene trusted him. Maybe they'd give him a chance.

"I've never forgotten you," it read. *"I don't ever want you to forget me."* And a small symbol at the bottom, one swirl of ink. The Ouroboros, biting its tail.

Selene began to shake, as if someone had thrown a bucket of cold water over their skin. Not Joshua. They sat down on the stool, hard enough to bruise, head in their hands, elbows on the work surface, trying to fight rising panic.

The flowers were from that fucking would-be rapist. Selene was sure of it.

Dangerdangerdanger. Selene's flight-or-freeze instincts warred inside them. They desperately wanted to run but could not move.

Selene forced themself to take a long, shaky breath in. Then a slow exhalation. Another inhalation, more steady this time. Selene was a witch. They knew how to breathe. They knew how to protect themselves, and damn it, they would find a way to get this man.

The words of the Moon Mother came back to them.

:Those who walk the pathways of darkness see into the night of other souls. Those who live in two worlds travel well. Seek the hidden pathway. See the truth.:

They still didn't know exactly what it meant, but figured if ever they needed to see into the night of other souls, it was now.

Maybe Selene didn't need the light of the full moon. Maybe they needed the small sickle moon, with its keen, sharp edge.

The knife they had just said they didn't want to be. But sometimes, the sharp edge was necessary.

They definitely needed the coven and its matron, Diana,

the huntress. She of the bow-shaped crescent.

Sitting up, breath finally slow and even, Selene pulled out their phone and sent a group text to the coven. *Alchemist just threatened me. Need to meet tonight.*

Then they texted Joshua. And Legis.

If the asshole was going to be this bold, they needed a planning meeting, and it had to happen ASAP.

Their phone buzzed. The first text was from Brenda. *Meet at shop? 7pm?*

With buzz after buzz, the coven chimed in. Pissed off as hell, they would be there.

Thank you, Mother.

Selene wasn't alone. Perhaps they never had been.

Looking at the roses, they throttled down the urge to dump them in one of the big garbage cans that dotted the space. They shouldn't. There might be a magical link there that someone in the coven could trace.

Selene sighed. There was no damn way they were going to be able to work now. Not with those blood red flowers sitting on their desk. They shoved tablet and phone back into their messenger bag. They should head to the hospital and check on Tabitha.

The damn flowers could stay in the car.

Selene packed up their things and slung their messenger bag cross-body. They bent over the bouquet, and grabbed the vase in both hands, ready to lift.

A wave of vertigo washed over them, and they sat on their chair with a whoosh of breath, scrabbling for a moment to keep the chair from rolling, and just saving the vase from tipping.

Focus. Focus.

Selene planted their boots on the floor, and bowed their head for a moment, still clutching the vase of roses. They slowed their breathing down behind the black curtain of their hair. Tuned in.

You're not going to get me, asshole, they thought, then expanded their awareness outward. Seeking.

There he was. The Alchemist. Selene got a clear image of him, in some sort of makeshift laboratory, using a dropper to transfer liquid from what looked like a test tube, and into an alembic. The fat-bellied alembic sat on a small blue gas fire.

The liquid was brown. They saw his head raise and look around. With a breath, Selene pulled their energy back. The scene changed. Tabitha. Floating. Limbs weakly churning the air around her, her head rolling back and forth, as if she was in distress.

The ropy brown cord emerged from Tabitha's navel area, and snaked its way through the æthers.

Where did the cord go?

The connection snapped, and Selene was thrown back in their chair. The vase rocked, water sloshing over the edge onto Selene's hands.

"Shit." They stabilized the vase again, and carefully removed their hands. There was really no throwing these roses away now. Tobias was going to need to see them. Lucy, too.

"You tried to trap me," Selene said, looking at the bloodred petals as they ripped tissues from a box, and wiped the table, the vase, and then their hands. "But you forgot that if you send something toward me, I can use it to get to *you*. Rookie mistake."

Selene looked around for something to wrap the vase in. It was clear they weren't going to be able to get it to their car if their skin touched any part of it. Then they remembered the gym towel in their locker cubby. It would do.

32

JOSHUA

Joshua banged on the glass door of the Inner Eye. Brenda looked up, tucking a wayward dark coil of hair behind one ear. Then she skirted the counter. The locks chunked in the door.

"Joshua, welcome back." She swept him into a hug that smelled of lavender and copal. She must have been burning that incense blend all day. One of the hazards of the magic worker was that they tended to smell of strange unguents and incenses. "How's your hand?"

"It's killing me. I just hope his face feels worse." Both things were true. Joshua wasn't used to physical confrontation, and his knuckles were abraded and bruised. Even his hand bones ached. "Everyone here?"

"Pretty much. I think we're just waiting on Lucy. Head back."

Joshua made his way to the purple Celtic-knot tapestry and pushed his way into the large class-slash-break room. Sure enough, beneath the brightly colored Elemental banners hanging from the walls in their respective directions, most of the chairs were filled. Including the two on either side of Selene. Damn.

He paused in the doorway for a moment, fingering the moonstone pendant in his pocket, searching for a chair. Legis waved at him from beneath the Fire banner on the southern side of the room. Frater Louis sat next to him and gave Joshua a look that seemed to see right through him. Something Joshua neither wanted or needed tonight.

Joshua gave a slight shake of his head and made a *just a moment* gesture. He drew the moonstone out and looked at Selene again. They were deep in conversation with Tobias and Raquel. He really shouldn't interrupt, but felt compelled to, all the same.

Brenda had said the moonstone pendant would act as a perfect focus for Selene. That was what he wanted, right? To give Selene something they could use in the coming battle? A tool to help them work their magic—magic he'd seen in action a couple of times over the past year; Selene was truly impressive—and hopefully a tool that would help to keep them safe.

And a gift that would let Selene know that Joshua was falling for them, hard. He wasn't sure how he felt about them knowing that. But it was just another part of daring, right?

Joshua took a deep breath and walked across the room. No time like the present.

Raquel saw him first, and fell silent, with one of those looks on her face as if she knew exactly what he was doing. What was up with these people tonight? Couldn't a guy get any privacy?

He knew the answer to that: Not when everyone's psychic senses were on high alert and he was probably broadcasting because he was agitated and in pain. His hand was really throbbing. He found it hard to care.

"Excuse me, Selene?"

They looked up, eyes flickering with so many different emotions, he couldn't tell what they were thinking.

"Hi Joshua." Their voice was a different timbre than before. A rich contralto. Gorgeous, just like the person speaking. The intimacy they'd shared the night before felt palpable, as if Joshua could touch it. Wrap it around himself.

"Oh my Goddess!" Tobias blurted out. "What happened to your hand?"

"I punched the Alchemist. I figured everyone would have heard. I saw Brenda this morning, and texted Selene, right after it happened."

Tobias paled. "No. No one said anything. But...we've been a little busy."

Tobias gestured toward the little kitchen area. A large vase of blood red roses stood on the counter next to the electric kettle. They looked menacing somehow, though Joshua couldn't pinpoint why.

"That present you texted me about? The Alchemist sent me roses," Selene remarked. "They're some sort of psychic trap. We want Lucy to see if there's anything else to be done with them."

"Well, damn." He turned to look at the flowers again. He had wanted to talk with Selene privately, but it was clear that was going to be too awkward to arrange. His neck burned beneath his starched collar. Damn it. People never affected him like this. Maybe he should just give them the moonstone some other time.

The pendant practically zapped his hand through the little satin bag.

"Joshua?" Selene asked.

How long had he just been standing there, half-turned, staring at the roses? He crouched down in front of Selene's chair, drawing the blue satin bag from his pocket.

"I, um. Got you something. A focus. I just...hoped it would help you with the magic."

He held out his hand, holding the small bag in his palm.

Selene's dark eyes looked into his, seeking something, then looked down at his hand. Their fingers snaked forward, brushing his hand, then withdrew, clutching the silk bag. Tipping the pendant from the bag, they inhaled sharply.

The moonstone glowed beneath the prosaic meeting room lights. It was suspended from a thick silver bow, the milky full moon partnered with the sickle of a waxing crescent. Selene's long, tapered fingers, stroked the pendant. Then they looked toward his face again.

"It's beautiful. Thank you."

"I thought it could maybe act as protection, too."

Selene nodded.

It was as if Tobias was gone. The rest of the coven was gone. The room itself was gone. It was just the two of them, and that little bit of magic Selene held in their hands.

Selene swept their black hair to one side, and unclipped one of the silver necklaces that cascaded in a fall down their chest. One of the shorter ones.

"It's cleansed?" they asked.

"Yes. Brenda smudged it in frankincense and benzoin for quite a while before she put it into the bag."

Selene nodded and threaded it onto the heavy chain.

"Would you?" they asked.

Joshua nodded, leaning forward, smelling the warmth of Selene's skin mixed with tuber roses, feeling their breath on his cheek. He grasped the two ends of the chain, and slid it around the pale column of Selene's neck. It took everything he had to not press his lips to the skin just beneath their chin, where it folded into their neck, dipping toward the black collar of their shirt. Instead, he inhaled, and thumbed the clasp open and shut, wincing as his bruised knuckles flexed.

Joshua paused for a moment before sliding his hands down the chain, and then parting, leaving Selene to occupy their own space again. He rocked back toward his own center of gravity, which suddenly didn't seem right anymore.

The pendant rested on Selene's breastbone. It already looked as if it had been there forever.

"Thank you, Joshua," Selene said. "For everything."

Joshua couldn't speak, so he simply squeezed Selene's hand, pushed up into a standing position, and looked around for an empty chair. Noise entered again. There were other people in the room. He heard people greeting someone. Lucy must have arrived.

He gave Selene a half smile, and turned toward the green north banner, where a couple of chairs sat, empty.

Moving away from Selene felt like walking upstream through a river.

"Hey, Joshua?" Selene called after him.

He turned.

"You should have Tobias or Tempest look at your hand."

"Yeah. That's probably a good idea," he said. Maybe when there was time. After all of this was over.

Lucy rushed past the curtain, followed by Brenda. Joshua took a seat.

"Okay," Tobias said, leaning forward in his chair, a lock of hair falling across his forehead. "Selene and I have cooked up a plan. What we need to do now is run it past all of you. Please try to poke holes in it. We need to not mess this one up. There's too much at stake. And after that, we'll figure out roles. Okay?"

Selene's fingers stroked the moonstone. They caught Joshua looking and gave him a slight smile before dropping their hand.

"Lucy," Selene said, "we already talked about the roses, and would love your take on them. Maybe you could check them out on a break?"

Lucy nodded as she swept her dark hair back into a ponytail. She'd come directly from work, if the paint stains on her pants and hands were any indication.

"What we'd like to do is use Tobias's dehydrator to quick-dry the rose petals so we can either use them as incense or to scatter on the ground. We'll have to see what feels right in the moment." Selene raised their hand, palm out. "And before you ask, yes, we'll use gloves, and yes, Tobias is willing to sacrifice the dehydrator if necessary."

"And what's this supposed to do?" Moss asked.

"Well, the roses linked me directly to the Alchemist, because he seems to be either stupid or uniformed. And then *he* led me to Tabitha. So...Tobias?"

Tobias took over the thread. "So we figure we can set a trap for him on the astral. Use his own magic against him."

"And?" Raquel asked.

"And then we shut him down," Selene replied. "Or take him out if necessary."

Joshua shivered a little. No one smiled. Everyone knew that if a witch talked like that, the situation was more than serious.

He knew then, without a doubt, that not only was Selene a total gorgeous badass, but he wanted to be just like the people in this room. Courageous, and knowing that magic would support them because they knew what they were doing.

And if people were in danger? They would move forward, regardless of the risks to themselves.

"We're already working with Quanice and the chaos magicians on disrupting the Alchemist's servitor," Frater Louis said.

"And the rest of us can run whatever containment or interference you need," Moss added.

Yeah. These people. These were the people Joshua wanted to surround himself with. As for his role in it all? He closed his eyes, and vowed to the strange Capricorn fish goat that he would do the best he could. And put his whole will and intention behind whatever was required.

I pledge my magic to these people, he thought. *And I pledge my life to magic.*

He was going to give it everything he had.

33

SELENE

It was six o'clock on a Friday evening, and a gorgeous day for the Trans March. The small heat wave had broken and the temperature was only in the high seventies. Big oaks and maples shaded the green grass and sidewalks of the North Park Blocks, a green space within the grid of four city blocks.

This was usually Selene's favorite day of the year. Oh, being in the midst of a crowd was never easy, and their protections had to be dialed up high, but seeing a glorious array of trans and non-binary people and their allies never failed to move Selene. It filled their heart with a sense of possibility that things could be okay for people like Selene. And mostly, that trans people and femmes wouldn't always have to live in what felt like constant danger.

Selene was a little bit nervous. This was the first time a magical operation Arrow and Crescent had planned felt so distinctly personal. Selene had never been a direct magical target before.

But they felt strong, too. Magically, they were as well

prepared as they were going to get, and were surrounded by their coven.

And Joshua was there, too. That fact simultaneously made Selene squirm with discomfort and want more. A lot more.

After he came to their apartment the night of the attack, something in Selene had relaxed, and decided he was safe. They touched the moonstone just beneath their collar bone. It felt right, as thought it had rested there for years.

"You okay?" Joshua asked. His lips buzzed near their ear, sending a good kind of shiver across Selene's skin.

Selene looked over at him and nodded. "I'm fine. I wish we could just enjoy the day, though. I wish people hadn't actually gotten hurt." And died.

"Yeah," he replied. There wasn't too much more to be said.

Joshua looked gorgeous, goatee freshly trimmed, top hat resting at a jaunty angle on his head. He wore a crisp white shirt under a burgundy vest. But Selene couldn't enjoy being in the park with *him*, either. There was work to be done.

They looked across the long squares of grass. Sandwiched between two stretches of Park and 8th, the grassy enclave was flanked by condos, art galleries, and restaurants, and was the starting place of many marches. Edging up against downtown, Chinatown, and the Pearl, it made a good gathering point.

Selene loved the big bronze Chinese elephant statue in the center of one of the blocks, with one small elephant standing on the back of one large. They could see them in the distance, one long block away. Two children pretended to ride the statue, watched carefully by two tall queens.

In the block not far from where the coven stood, was a

white pop-up shelter with a small sound system and some folding chairs set up beneath. A regal-looking Black trans woman spoke into the microphone about the threats trans women of color faced every day.

Selene felt cold, despite the warm day. Their own attack was still with them, and the threat was still out there. They were white, and non-binary, but as a femme-presenting person, the risks were real. And for Black and brown trans women? The threats were amplified.

A Chinese American trans woman walked by, holding aloft a big sign that read "Yellow Peril for Black Lives." Members of the Portland Two-Spirit Society were present, some wearing elaborate beadwork; others, bright shawls. Some of them carried stiff fans made of dark brown feathers.

Damn the Alchemist for ruining this beautiful day.

Brenda and Raquel, heads close, conferred about something, while Tobias and Moss unfurled a big banner that read *Queer Witches Support Our Trans and NB Siblings* with a big pentacle smack in the center. The other coven members were clumped nearby. They were hoping to stay put at the beginning of the march. It was going to be easier and simpler to do magic if they were all in one place. Selene didn't trust that the whole coven could stay together once the crowd began to move.

Plus, some of the members felt they should not join the march, being only supporters and allies. That decision made sense, but Selene was pretty clear that if the asshole Alchemist showed up, the way they thought he would, the coven was doing whatever the hell was necessary. If that meant marching, they would march.

"Do you sense him anywhere?" Selene asked Joshua.

Besides Selene, Joshua and Lucy had the closest energetic links to the man.

Joshua shook his head. "No. But that could just be because there are so many people here."

A discordant ripple came from Selene's left, toward the edge of this block. Shouting. People running.

"Let's go!" That was Alejandro, taking off, Tempest and Cassiel right behind. Selene followed the purple of Tempest and the bright red of Cassiel, both women's hair sparking each time the sun hit as they passed in and out of shade.

"Selene!" Joshua called out. They didn't care. They had to see what was happening. Every ache in their body flared. Joshua was right, they shouldn't have been running into danger. But that was what the coven was here for, wasn't it? To confront the Alchemist.

The Sisters of Perpetual Indulgence had formed a cordon of giant rainbow flags and blue-and-pink trans pride flags stretched taut between tall poles. Their wimples and veils towered, glittering and gleaming in the sun on the street. Above their flag-and-pole partition fences rose banners with giant painted flames, and words condemning everyone to hell.

God Hates You read one of the banners.

Well, wasn't that special. The Alchemist wasn't the only asshole they had to be on the lookout for today.

Selene stopped, chest heaving, still not fully recovered from the attack. Joshua stopped next to them, also gasping. Just because the nicotine hadn't had much time to affect him, didn't mean he'd come out unscathed.

"Are those Fred Phelps' people?" he asked, once he caught his breath and plopped his top hat back on his head.

"Looks that way. I forgot they usually show up for Pride and try to make us feel as ashamed as possible."

Joshua grinned and wiped sweat from his face with a fancy handkerchief. "How's that working out?"

Selene barked out a startled laugh. "Pretty well for us, not so well for them."

Alejandro, Tempest, and Cassie had doubled back and hooked up with them.

"I don't understand what they get out of this," Alejandro said. He looked neat as a pin, even after the sprint across the park. His shirt today was rainbow-striped, for pride. Selene always forgot he was bisexual, because he'd dated only women for as long as Selene had been in the coven. They kicked themself for forgetting.

"Oh, people like that just love to feel superior," Tempest replied. "Jerks."

"We should get back to the rest of the coven," Selene said. "I'm not feeling too good about this situation all of a sudden."

"Is he here?" Alejandro asked, face serious, body posture tense, clearly on high alert.

Selene closed their eyes for a moment, trying to sense the edges of the park, then opened them again.

They looked at their coven mate.

"I don't know," they said. "But something doesn't feel right. I just want us all back in one place."

"Let's go," Cassiel said, and turned. Selene followed the bright banner of her red hair through the increasing crowd, making sure the energy still cycled around the edge of their aura, keeping the excited and happy crush of emotions and thoughts at bay.

34

JOSHUA

J oshua didn't care about anything right now except finding the Alchemist. That wasn't his official job in this operation, but it was a job he felt prepared to do. The connection to tobacco was still with him, which was one good outcome from the poisoning. He and Lucy both had that now, but Lucy wasn't here. She had offered to sit with Tabitha in the hospital today, to make sure the woman was magically safe. Joshua just hoped it was enough.

Several coven members had an intuition that the Alchemist was going to strike during the Trans March. It made sense. If the asshole thought that Selene, as a non-binary person, was a "perfect alchemical creature," then he was going to want to be in a place where there were sure to be non-binary people gathering. The trans march was open to trans, non-binary, and gender fluid people and their families and friends. And trans and enby people tended toward mutual support.

Besides, the Alchemist also seemed to be targeting queer people and artists in general. Maybe it was some strange attempt to fire up the alchemical philosopher's stone, reaching enlightenment, turning the base metal of his life into gold. For a megalomaniac that probably looked a great deal like becoming king of the world.

Add in the powerful energy of an excited crowd, and the Trans March was going to be catnip for the man.

Joshua followed Selene and Cassiel back to the rest of Arrow and Crescent. The crowd was growing. Joshua wasn't used to a crush of bodies on anything other than a dance floor. He wove his way between two gorgeous women in slim summer dresses, wondering how in the world they were going to march in those heels.

The skin on his right hand tingled. The energetic trace of the nicotine activating. The Alchemist must be near.

"Excuse me," Joshua said to two trans men in matching pink shirts and straw boaters. He pushed forward, trying to keep pace with Selene, who strode across the grass as if they owned the place.

Selene on the verge of magical battle was impressive. There was no hint of the shy awkwardness that so often colored how they walked in the world. This Selene was a Valkyrie. A badass wizard. A virago.

They were so gorgeous, Joshua thought his heart might stop. Truly. They wore the moonstone pendant today. The large piece, topped by a silver crescent moon, seemed to vibrate. Watching their black hair stream behind as they strode through the crowd, shirt swirling, boot buckles shining beneath black jeans, Joshua was struck.

He was in love.

Was that what the feeling was? It had to be. It wasn't the sense that the Alchemist was near. His heart wasn't racing from nicotine. Not right now.

His heart raced for Selene.

Sap, he thought. He shook his head and forged on, finally close enough to touch Selene's shoulder.

"Hey," he said, just loud enough for his voice to reach their ears. He touched their shoulder, feeling the warmth beneath the long, loose black shirt that flowed around their body. Selene's head turned. Their eyes caught his. He noticed that their eyeliner was slightly smudged beneath their left eye. Their lips were red today. The red of the blood of their enemies.

Selene slowed down. Joshua matched their step.

"I feel him," he said.

"The Alchemist?"

"Yes. The skin on my hand feels funny, from where the ointment touched it."

Selene looked around, scanning the crowd. Joshua felt their aura as it...shifted. Expanded? Softened? He couldn't quite pinpoint it, but Selene was definitely scanning with more than just their eyes.

"Can you tell where he is?" they finally asked. "It feels like somewhere on the northwest corner, but I'm getting a lot of interference."

Use what you've got. The basics, remember?

He slowed his breathing down, and imagined a candle flame in front of him. Centering on that image, he softened, and allowed his own senses to expand. Seeking out the thread that connected him to the spirit of tobacco. To the nicotine. Seeking out the Alchemist.

"Come on...show me where you are," he whispered across the park.

The whole park seemed to flip, as if the world turned upside down and back again, not landing in exactly the same orientation as before.

"What the hell was that?" Joshua heard Moss ask.

Joshua blinked. Had they somehow walked all the way back to the rest of the coven already? Sure enough, there were Tobias and Moss holding the *Queer Witches* banner and the rest of the coven as well. Raquel nodded at him, and Brenda waved. Frater Louis was there, too, in a bright purple button-up shirt. Legis stood next to him, wearing a black T-shirt that read *I'll Mess Up Anyone Who Messes With You.*

Quanice and some of his friends had arrived. *Queer Chaotes in Solidarity With Our Trans Siblings* their banner read. In the center of the banner was the black chaos star, its bristle of arrows pointing outward from the center.

But what about that flipping sensation? Where was the Alchemist and what was he doing?

"No, no... He's not northwest," he said to Selene. "That's a blind. He must have backup, setting up decoys or something." Joshua cast outward again, seeking. Following the thread. Gotcha.

"He's back at the bronze elephants," Joshua said, opening his eyes again.

"How in the world?" Selene asked.

"He flipped the park somehow," Joshua said.

Raquel spoke. "He must be doing time and space shift magic. Probably has a servitor for it."

She turned toward the chaos magicians.

"Quanice?"

Quanice handed his edge of the banner to one of his cohort and stepped forward. Today's outfit was red high-top Chuck Taylors, a red T-shirt with a chaos star in the center, and black jeans.

"Yes ma'am."

"Don't call me ma'am," Raquel said. "I'm nowhere near old enough. Do you work with any time or space servitors?"

Quanice grinned. "I sure do."

"Can you help us reverse whatever this guy's doing?" Joshua asked.

Quanice thought for a moment.

"I can't do that. But we can call on a servitor to get you in."

"Get us in?" Selene asked.

Quanice smiled again. "Yeah. If you give us a minute to figure out what operation they're running, we can probably find a way to slide you in between the place where space and time connect."

"You can do that?" Raquel sounded impressed.

No shit. That was pretty impressive if Quanice's crew could actually pull it off.

"Only one way to find out," Quanice replied. "Let me talk to the crew."

35

SELENE

As Raquel and Brenda strategized with the rest of the coven and the other magicians gathered there, Selene and Tobias took a moment to confer. They had asked him for a moment and he waited, tapping at a mullein leaf with one finger. Why mullein? Selene didn't know. It must be some herbalist thing. Tobias always had something in his pockets these days.

Selene closed their eyes for a moment, breathing in the scents and sounds and energies of the park. They could practically taste the Alchemist. Swallowing down bile, they re-centered. Wiggled toes in their buckle boots, rocking back and forth on the grass. Grounding. They couldn't be off for this. It was too important. While there was no telling what exactly would happen, or whether the trap they'd made would even work, Selene had to be ready for what was to come.

Because something *was* coming. The whole stretch of the park blocks, despite the festive aura, thrummed with it. Whatever the Alchemist was doing rippled through every pocket of music, laughter, weirdness, and agitation. Selene hoped the Sisters of Perpetual Indulgence were ready for it, and not too distracted by the hateful street preachers they currently contended with. Alejandro had talked with Sister Krissy, giving a heads-up, but since he couldn't tell them exactly what to look for, Krissy just said that the Sisters would be ready to offer protection to whomever needed it. That was what the flag walls were there for, and knowing the Sisters, those flag walls were imbued with a little something extra.

Selene had a sudden flash, an image of Lucy sitting at Tabitha's bedside. They hoped both women were all right. Lucy looked up, as if she could see Selene, then shook her head and gestured Selene away.

Don't distract yourself, their coven sister mouthed. *I got this.*

Selene snapped their attention back to the park blocks. Back to Joshua, standing at their side, smelling of amber undercut with the slightest tang of sweat and fear.

"Hey," they said, touching his white shirt. "Are you okay?"

He swallowed, then cupped Selene's cheek. The look in his eyes made Selene want to weep, and they didn't know why.

"I'm okay," he said. "Part of me feels calm. Ready. But the other part? I have to be honest with you, Selene."

He leaned in closer. They breathed together for one long moment, forgetting the park, the Alchemist, the crush of people....

"I'm terrified that something is going to happen to you and I won't be able to help." Joshua paused, then dropped his hand to Selene's shoulder. Soft. Warm. Gentle. "And I know...I'm falling for you, okay? So, do what you have to do, but please be careful if you can."

Heat slid up Selene's neck. Their cheeks grew hot. They wrestled down their impulse to run. Planted their boots in the grass for what must have been the thirteenth time that day. *Stay, Selene. Please stay,* they thought. Selene realized then that they'd never wanted anything more. Than to stay. To allow their body to lean into this man, their hands to reach up. Touch his jaw.

Draw him closer. Look into his eyes.

"Okay," Selene replied.

A throat cleared behind them.

"I'm sorry to interrupt," Moss said, "but Tobias needs you. He thinks it's time."

Selene took one step back. Joshua stood, stock-still, eyes trained on their face. Selene's lips turned up into a smile.

They turned to Moss then, who was all kitted out for battle. Black bandana around his neck. Old *Earth First!* T-shirt hugging his skinny frame, gripping the *Queer Witches* banner as if it was going to be ripped from his hands.

Selene wasn't yet sure if they loved Joshua, but they loved Moss. Loved everyone in Arrow and Crescent. Their coven. Their family.

The thing they would fight and die for.

"Let's do this," Selene said.

Tobias had the one jar of ointment they'd managed to save, planning to use it as a physical anchor to the Alchemist if needed. Selene's hands itched to hold it, but Tobias wanted to make sure everything else was in place before handing it over. He also had a paper sack of dried rose petals.

"I don't trust this situation, Selene," Tobias said, stroking his goatee. "There's too many variables. Too much can go wrong."

His dark hair flopped over his face and his lips turned

down in a frown. Dressed in battered gray chinos and sneakers, he wore a rainbow unicorn T-shirt as a concession that this was supposed to be a fun weekend.

Not so much. Damn the Alchemist for ruining everyone's Pride.

People are dead, Selene, they chided themself. Selene shook their head. A long dark strand stuck to their lips, embedded in the bloodred lipstick they'd slicked on half an hour before. People were sick and even dead, and now this crowd—gathered because they wanted nothing more than a chance to be festive together on a sunny day—was in possible danger.

The trans and enby communities had too much stolen from them already. Any chance to reaffirm life was one they needed to take. But this bastard was trying to steal that away, too. Anger flashed through Selene's body. It was time to become the Goddess's blade again.

Breath shuddered into their lungs and certainty sliced through them.

"We can't always get a clear read, Tobias. You know that. But if we're going to attack, it has to be today. Now."

"What I mean is," Tobias said, voice edging toward impatience, "I don't trust that this isn't all some elaborate ruse to snare *you.* We need to be even more careful than usual. I am *not* feeding you directly into his hands."

"Well, I *am* the fabled alchemical creature, haven't you heard?"

"Stop it." Joshua stepped up beside Selene. "Never call yourself by a name that man used. Don't give him that power."

Selene sighed. "I'm not giving him any power. Trust me. The man is an idiot."

"An idiot who managed to convince a whole bunch of

people to give him money and time. An idiot who has taken out several of our friends. An idiot..." Tobias started ranting.

Selene put a hand on his arm. "Tobias. I get that you're scared. But I can't be, okay? Just let me do my thing."

Brenda and Raquel came back over.

"You almost ready?" Raquel asked. "The rest of the coven is primed to put the protections up. Louis and Legis are anchoring the whole thing. We just need to check with Quanice. Make sure the Chaotes are ready, too."

"I'm not ready," Tobias said. He was sweating.

"Well, you have to *get* ready," Selene said, a sudden flare of anger flashed through their body. "I can't hold on much longer, Tobias. The power is building. Can't you feel it?"

The energy ramped up and all of a sudden, Selene felt as if they were in a movie or something. They swore their hair must be swirling around their head, and felt as if they were levitating off the grass. The sounds of the crowd around the little pocket of magic workers sounded like the roaring of a mighty ocean, ready to crash upon a vast shore.

Everything wobbled, throwing them off center. The energy at the edges of their aura felt brittle, close to fracturing.

"Raquel?" they said.

"What do you need?" Raquel's voice sounded like steel coated with honey. Selene needed some of that.

"I can't ground. It's all too strong."

Selene felt Raquel's hands on their shoulders and heard Raquel's voice in their left ear.

"Take a breath all the way from the crown of your head to the soles of your feet."

Selene tried to comply. They fought to drop their attention into center. Fought to take a breath that would fill their whole body with the flow of oxygen. They felt the moon, just past full now, waning one sliver a day. The sun was waning, too. Just barely.

They felt the sun and moon together in the sky, mighty cosmic forces. And ordinary, too. The magic of a reflective rock and a combustible star. Night and day. Selene felt it so clearly, this dance.

"The sun and moon must marry one another. Together, they shall have a child, and name that child Aradia." Another alchemical wedding. They'd never thought of it that way before.

Selene didn't know if they had spoken the words aloud or not, but they must have, because they felt Raquel's hands press more firmly downward, toward the earth. Then Brenda stepped in front of them.

"Selene," Brenda said. "You need to stay with us until it is time. You're already too far out. Ground and center. Reinforce your own boundary. Hold fast."

Mother Moon...

"I *can't.*"

"Does anyone have some tiger iron?" Brenda's head whipped back and forth.

"I do," Tempest said, proffering a lump of tumbled stone, striations of deep gray hematite interlaced with tiger stripes of warm orangey browns.

Brenda slid the stone into Selene's right hand. Selene lurched sideways, then took in a ragged breath. Felt their eyes flutter. Felt their soul sink toward their feet again. The energies around them dialed down, from ten to around seven. Still vibrant, slightly over the top, but manageable. The sounds in the park normalized, voices, laughter, drums become distinct noises once again. Sunlight winked and flashed among the leaves.

"Thank you," they said to Brenda.

Raquel's hands released their shoulders.

"I want you to hold onto the stone until you need to fly. It would be my preference that you keep it, but I understand you may need more freedom from the earth plane." Brenda made sure Selene was looking directly at her before continuing. "You're one of the strongest sorcerers in this coven. You are *not* expendable. You are coming back to us, no matter what, you hear?"

Raquel stood next to Brenda, arms crossed over her chest, and gave a firm nod.

"Okay. I'm okay," Selene replied. It wasn't quite an acknowledgement that they understood. But they did understand. All too well. They just weren't one-hundred percent in agreement. They would come back if they could. But if it was necessary not to? They would do what it took.

But they weren't going to tell Brenda or Raquel that.

Cassiel walked up and handed Selene a water bottle of coated red steel, top already screwed off. Selene took a drink, then handed the bottle back.

"Tobias and I are ready," Cassiel said. "You okay?"

"Fine," Selene said. "Let's trap this asshole."

They sent a thought toward Lucy, letting her know to be on alert, and felt an affirmative.

It was about to go down.

Selene slipped the stone into their pocket, then turned. "Where's Joshua?"

36

JOSHUA

Joshua had decided that he was going to take the fish goat by the horns and try to stop this thing before it started.

If he could take out the Alchemist physically, before Selene and Tobias even set their magical trap? Maybe he could eliminate the threat, and this crowd could enjoy the rest of the day without an invisible sword hanging over their heads.

Leaving the experts to help ground Selene, he walked over to where Legis, Frater Louis, and Quanice's chaos magician buddies were clustered behind the banner emblazoned with the chaos star. Frater Louis and Quanice gestured at one another, clearly engaged in an intense conversation.

"No," Quanice was saying, "you can't just cut the cord between a magician and their servitor! Do you know how much could go wrong?"

"So what do you suggest we do?" Frater Louis replied. His voice was calm, but the small Thelemite was practically vibrating with energy. Everyone was ready for battle.

Joshua tapped Legis on the shoulder.

"Hey," Joshua said.

Legis bent his head toward Joshua. "What's up?"

"I'm going to do something that may be stupid."

"And what, you want backup?"

Joshua considered. He did want backup. But Legis already had a role...

"I would love backup, but don't you need to anchor this whole thing?"

Legis huffed. "Are you kidding? Frater Louis can stabilize the whole operation while dancing a jig and fighting off dogs."

"That's...quite an image."

"So, what's the plan?"

"I want to find the Alchemist and take him out before anything starts."

Legis crossed his arms over his big chest, and raised his right eyebrow.

"You mean, physically?" he asked.

"Yeah. I punched him once already, and I'm not even any good. And you're big. I think we can do this."

Legis nodded. "I didn't expect this from you, but okay. I'm in."

The big Thelemite turned and interrupted Frater Louis and Quanice.

"We're going on a mission. Hopefully we'll be back before we're needed, but just in case, Frater Louis, can you hold this thing together on your own?"

Frater Louis gave Legis a look as though he knew they were up to no good. He pursed his lips and finally shrugged.

"Do what you need to do," Louis said. "If we don't have enough firepower and experience from this crew? This whole thing is going to fail anyway. We may as well approach it from every angle we can."

"Let's go," Legis said.

Joshua took one last look at Selene, who was still absorbed with Tobias, Brenda, and Raquel.

I love you, he thought.

Then he and Legis headed toward the center of the first park block, winding through the bright crowd.

I hope I'm doing the right thing.

He had invoked Éliphas Lévi's Power to Dare and it seemed as if that was all he was doing today. Taking risks.

He and Legis started walking, heading toward the bronze elephants.

"You got a plan?" Legis asked over his shoulder as he cut a swathe through the crowd.

"Trip him? Shove his face into the ground?" Joshua replied. He was regretting wearing his top hat. He hadn't figured on wanting to get into a fistfight with this guy.

It was as if some flip-side Joshua had taken over. A man who used his fists instead of his charm.

There was just no charming some people.

Legis slowed down a bit, letting Joshua catch up. "You say he's by the elephants?"

"I think so. He's pulling some space-time weirdness so it's still hard to tell, but that's where I felt him the strongest."

They were stopped several yards from the fanciful statue, and the crowd was even more dense than before. But this close to the stacked elephants, Joshua could see that there was actually a small clearing to one side. And the children who had been playing on the structure earlier were gone.

"Look at that. He's got to be there."

They rounded the bulk of the statue and sure enough, there was the Alchemist in a top hat of his own today, and a peacock-colored waistcoat that Joshua would have envied in other circumstances. A white shirt. Black trousers.

Surrounding him were three blond, middle-aged, middle-class-looking women, a portly man with dark hair, and a young, shirtless skinny white man in rainbow trousers. The women and the portly man seemed as if they were holding up a circle. Joshua softened his gaze and saw it. It was as if the air bent slightly around them, cordoning off the space.

The shirtless man lay down in the center.

"Oh no. Nononono. That is so not good," Joshua said, increasing his speed.

"How are we going to get in there?" Legis asked, jerking Joshua to a stop. "We have to think for a minute, man."

"Joshua!" Selene's voice rang across the park. The fact that he heard it over the noise of the crowd was a miracle. He turned and saw them striding across the park, hair flying, electric, looking like an avenging angel. They were flanked by the whole coven, and the chaos magicians, banners tangling in legs, everyone rushing his way. His mouth went dry and his heart pounded in his chest.

"Joshua!" Legis said. "Look!"

Joshua ripped his gaze from Selene and turned back to the weird circle just east of the elephant.

The Alchemist was smearing something all over the shirtless man. It gleamed in the dappled evening sun.

Flying ointment.

"Shit."

37

SELENE

Damn Joshua and Legis for taking off on their own. That was *not* the agreement they'd made. What the hell were they planning? Selene just hoped it wasn't something physical, not in the middle of a bunch of people who hadn't asked for this fight. Who had just shown up, wanting to celebrate Pride, and be around a bunch of people who celebrated *them*, for one damn day out of the year.

But they had no time to deal with that. The Alchemist had turned for a moment when Selene called out to Joshua, and stared straight at them across the distance, his hands shining with flying ointment. How was he protected from it? That was strange. Maybe the batches he used with his own people had less nicotine?

He had looked at Selene with desire before turning to the half-naked man lying on the ground. The Alchemist's gaze turned Selene's stomach. They fought the bile down. Again.

Focus. You have a lot of people counting on you. Why was magic so much more difficult the more personal it became?

"Tobias," Selene said. Their coven mate stood at Selene's

shoulder. "Can you get a bead on that ointment? How is he using it?"

Tobias reached for their hand. Selene grabbed hold, and felt his aura shift sideways, seeking outward. Their own aura flared, then subsided. They should really distract the Alchemist.

The chaos magicians, Moss, and Cassiel must have had the same idea, because they were moving swiftly, banners flapping against their legs as they moved toward the shimmering sphere next to the elephant, and faced outward, stretching the banners tight. That was good: the elephants blocked the western view of the Alchemist's circle, and the banners would keep people away from north and east. The magicians and witches had left the southern quadrant of the circle open, so Selene and the others could do their work. That included Quanice, whom Selene really hoped had gotten a bead on the servitor.

As if he had heard, Quanice stepped to Selene's other side.

"Tobias scoping things out?" he asked.

"He's trying to figure out why the ointment isn't killing the Alchemist. How did you guys do with the tobacco servitor?"

Quanice rubbed his chin. "Since we figured out the connection yesterday, we should be good to go whenever you and Tobias are. And Lucy knows what to do, too. As for the space-time shit, we can definitely get you in. Just let me know when, and we'll open the path."

Selene nodded and licked their lips. The Alchemist paced, agitated, around his sphere, pushing outward with his hands. The witches and magicians swayed, and then grew still again as he passed. He must be trying to push them out of his way. They responded by rooting more deeply in the earth. He clearly had never encountered anyone who knew how to work actual magic, instead of just going through the motions.

"We're ready to go. So are Raquel and Brenda and the rest." Quanice gestured toward Tobias, who stood preternaturally still, eyes closed. "How long do you think he'll be?"

"I'm back." Tobias rolled his head and rotated his shoulders. "As far as I can tell, you're right, the ointment he's using has less nicotine in it than the samples he gave away. Enough to form a connection, but not enough to cause real damage. I think we need to go ahead. That guy on the ground is already flying. Shit's happening on the astral, big time."

Selene raised their voice, just slightly. "Arrow and Crescent?"

The coven gathered closer, so did the rest of the Chaotes.

"Tobias and I are going in. You all ready to back us up?"

Raquel stepped in front of Selene, dark eyes searching Selene's face, Alejandro right beside her. Selene could tell he was reading their aura. That was fine. In situations like this, coven members knew they always had permission.

"How do you want to proceed?" Raquel finally said.

"I *want* to bust through that damn sphere and wrap my fingers around his neck. But what we're going to do is get up on the astral and disrupt his operation before he hurts anyone else. Just as planned."

"Good," Raquel said.

"Shall we?" they said to Tobias. He nodded, and they both sat down on the grass.

"May I?" Quanice asked.

Selene nodded. He placed his warm hands on their temples, then spoke.

"I'm going to show you the image of a door. It's up to you to take Tobias through."

Selene slowed their breathing down, and turned their attention inward for a moment, one hand holding the moonstone pendant. The horns of the silver crescent pressed into their hand. *I feel you, Mother.* Then they allowed their gaze to shift again, opening out, widening their perspective to include the astral planes, the æthers.

There it was, a shimmering, golden doorway.

"Let's go, Tobias."

"Ready," he said, slipping his hand into theirs. And, lifting slowly from their bodies, they both flew toward the door.

Selene barreled through it in a rush, Tobias trailing just behind. A sonic boom flung them backwards. They cheated left, so they wouldn't be blown back through the doorway, and fought to stabilize their ætheric body and slow the trajectory down.

Quanice hadn't been joking. Things were literally blowing up on this plane. What in the world was the Alchemist even trying? Shrapnel flew by. Pieces of what looked like a snake's body, bird feathers, shards of glass. Selene dodged as best as they could. There was no telling what sort of effect the objects would have on their astral form. And how any injuries on this plane would affect their body on the ground.

Speaking of, they really hoped someone was guarding them and Tobias. That *had* been Joshua's job.

:*Tobias?*: Selene sent the thought out toward their coven mate.

:*Here.*: The thought returned, and Tobias zoomed up next to them. :*You okay?*:

:*Fine. What next? Is everything set with the roses?*:

:Yes. Brenda and Raquel have them. They should deploy them any time now. We'll feel it when that happens.:

Selene nodded, and took stock. In order to trap the Alchemist, the coordination between physical plane and the astral was going to have to be almost seamless. Add in whatever Lucy was going to need to do, and this whole operation felt...

Like the stakes were too damn high.

:We just need to move.: Selene sent the thought toward Tobias. A witch could only plan an operation like this so far, then it was off script, using nothing but skill, intuition, and whatever tools they had on hand.

They had to trust that it would be enough.

38

JOSHUA

Joshua could tell by the look on their face that Selene was pissed off, but they'd stopped with the rest of the coven before getting close enough to even talk. And then Moss and Cassiel, and a couple of the chaos magicians had rolled past with their big banners, stationing themselves around the weird space-time sphere, leaving a gap in the south.

Things looked ready to go down.

"What do we do now?" he asked Legis. "Do you think we can still break through the sphere?"

The Thelemite considered. "Maybe. The real question is, should we? Now that Selene and Tobias are here, is it going to mess things up? Make things worse?"

"I'm still hoping we can stop this thing before it starts."

Legis gestured toward the man on the ground, who had begun trembling, as if he lay on top of his own private earthquake. "I think it's already started, man."

So what were they supposed to do? Joshua keenly felt his lack of discipline and training. He could have been training for this moment for years. Instead? He'd been wallowing in his own particular brand of self-pity and avoidance.

Well, damn it, he was going to show up now.

Capricorn, devil, whatever you are, if you want me to harness my will to my desire and set myself free, help me now. I desire this more than I have anything in the last five years. I desire magic. And responsibility. Give me what you've got. See me through.

A burst of energy filled his limbs. The aches and pains from the poisoning and punching the Alchemist were still present, but they didn't matter anymore. His head cleared. He knew what he had to do.

Taking in three deep breaths, he fortified the edges of his aura, making them as seamless and strong as he could. Then he turned to Legis.

"Let's go," Joshua said, and barreled toward that wide open southern quadrant. Extending his aura outward like a wedge, he slammed into the shimmering edge of the sphere.

39

———

SELENE

Selene held the image of the tobacco servitor in their head, and calibrated their vision again, trying to tune out the static. That was all the booms and astral debris were: static. Something to keep them occupied while the Alchemist did his nasty work.

How Selene knew this, they wouldn't be able to explain. They began to move, rising on the planes, using the magical hook he'd placed in them—likely way back when he'd roofied their drink—to track his location on the astral.

There. A cul de sac just off this second ætheric plane. Selene realized now that the first plane they'd passed through had been a construct, which was some pretty crafty magic. It wasn't on the actual astral at all, but a psychic airlock, designed to keep people out. It must have been a safety set into whatever lock he'd put on the space-time magic, and when Quanice punched a door through, it had brought them to a place that was no place at all.

Got you now, bastard. Selene knew the astral like the back of their well-manicured hand. They stepped out into a rolling, light gray fog, Tobias right behind them, and walked with certainty toward where they felt the Alchemist to be. He tugged on them the way a lover might, and that just pissed Selene off. He had no right to their body, no right to their mind, no right to their soul.

Selene walked through the misty veil, and there he was. He towered here, his astral image as inflated as his ego. But instead of the peacock colors he'd clothed himself in, here, his aura was filled with shades of brown and gray. A miasma of tobacco juice and uncertainty.

Well, well, well. Wasn't that funny? He didn't know what the hell he was doing, did he? He had just convinced the greater part of himself he did. And convinced other people, too. Because otherwise, he would collapse in an insecure heap on the floor.

Selene smiled. They knew that feeling all too well, that sense of insecurity and not knowing. So they could use it as a weapon and a curse.

And magic was the one thing Selene never felt insecurity about. Their Goddess had made sure of that. Waxing or waning, crescent or full, Selene's magic was always there.

The tobacco servitor scuttled back and forth, back and forth. It seemed agitated. Unhappy. Skeins of brown radiated from its stumpy torso, heading off in all directions. Selene was surprised it could even move, there were so many threads feeding off of it.

Or feeding back *into* it. That was why it was agitated. It was taking in life force from all the people it was connected to. It was an over-capacity battery, almost full to bursting.

Selene's moonstone began to glow, beaming a soft radiance outward. Tobias's aura must have been glowing, too, because a wash of green tinged the air. They didn't want to risk a look, holding their gaze steady on the Alchemist and the servitor.

The Alchemist's head snapped toward Selene and Tobias, attracted by the glow. He grinned his sick grin.

"You've come," he said. "And you brought a friend."

Selene was glad he spoke instead of sending thoughts, because they really didn't want his oily voice inside their head. They felt a tug on the connection, and allowed themself to be drawn toward him.

The trap had been set, so carefully, by Tobias and Selene.

And Selene was the trap.

40

JOSHUA

Smashing into the Alchemist's sphere was like barreling into plate glass. It shattered around him, loud as a car crash. The front edge of his aura tore away in ribbons. He felt as if his skin was on fire. Head pounding, skin screaming, he rolled inside the sphere, slamming to the grass. Legis bounced beside him, groaning.

"Fuck," the big magician said.

Joshua staggered to his feet, pressing his hands to his head.

The Alchemist stood beside the half-naked man. Eyes closed, his hands gestured, making sigils in the air.

"Hold the sphere!" he shouted. His minions scurried, panicked, trying to shore up the broken container. One of the men moved toward Joshua and kicked outward. Joshua dodged. The man's boot passed his knee.

As if on cue, the chaos magicians began skipping in a circle around the elephants and the people holding banners and the now-shattered sphere.

"Ring around the rosy! Pockets full of posies! Ashes, ashes, all fall *down*!" On and on they went, skipping, cackling, and singing in a sunwise circle. The power they raised bowed outward, containing the broken sphere, and edging another layer of protection outward. They were keeping the crowd safe.

Joshua sensed Selene flying on the æthers, and sent a distracted thought upward. The man closed in and threw a roundhouse punch, telegraphing the move from a mile away. Joshua blocked the punch with an outward wave of his arm.

Wax off, he thought.

"Ring around the rosy! Pockets full of posies! Ashes, ashes, all fall *down!*"

The man was sweating, face a sickly red that edged toward purple. His fist snapped toward Joshua's chin. Joshua deflected again—*Wax on*—before throwing a punch of his own.

From the corner of his eye, he caught Brenda walking, counterclockwise, scattering something on the ground. The rose petals.

"Ring around the rosy! Pockets full of posies! Ashes, ashes, all fall *down!*"

Legis appeared behind the man and clocked him on the temple. The man fell like a stone.

Drumming started up nearby, laying down a beat over at the far edge of park near Burnside. A brass band began to play, syncopating with the beat. Michael Jackson's "Wanna Be Starting Something."

People began moving toward the band. The march must be starting.

"Ring around the rosy! Pockets full of posies! Ashes, ashes, all fall *down!*"

Brenda finished her circuit with the roses, and threw a last handful into the air. It flew into the center of the circle, showering Joshua and Legis, the Alchemist and his minions. Petals stuck to the gleaming ointment on the supine man's chest.

As the Alchemist flung his hands skyward, Joshua and Legis sprung toward him. Legis crashed into the man's chest, arms wrapping around his torso. Joshua aimed low, and slammed into his thighs. They all fell in a whoosh, crashing down onto the man on the ground, then rolled and smacked the grass. Hard. Joshua's teeth snapped together.

"Ring around the rosy! Pockets full of posies! Ashes, ashes, all fall *down*!"

A huge *crack!* split the air before the excited crowd and the brass of the band drowned it out again.

41

SELENE

Selene heard a cracking sound and felt the astral shift. The Alchemist stumbled and fell. The servitor stopped its frenetic back and forth. For the first time, it looked directly at Selene.

:*Come here?*: Selene thought.

:*Why should I?*: it beamed back.

:*I can free you.*:

And Selene could. They were certain of it.

The Alchemist rolled and shot a twining brown cord at Selene. They grabbed for it with their right hand and it snapped against their palm, leaving a stinging welt. Selene hissed, closed their astral fingers, and held on.

:*I just felt Brenda deploy the roses*: Tobias sent. :*I'm ready, too.*:

:*As above, so below,*: Selene responded, then turned their attention back to the servitor.

:*Ready?*: they thought, and threw an image into the servitor's head. A twining. A binding. A shattering.

A plan.

:—: They felt an affirmative from the servitor. :*Then free?*:

:Then free.:

:Tobias, stand ready.:

Selene tightened their grip on the thick brown cord and touched the moonstone amulet with the other hand. The Alchemist's magic. Their magic. One of those would prevail.

They tuned into the astral essence of the moonstone, then called upon the power of the moon, and its twin, the sun. Selene was ready.

They would stand now, exposed in all their power, in all their glory, without shame. Everything aligned within them and around them, resonating through all the worlds.

They raised their arms—"Now!" they shouted into the churning mist—then sliced them downward.

The servitor ran in rings around the Alchemist, binding him with the brown tobacco cords.

The Alchemist struggled against his own creation.

"What are you *doing*? You little *shit*! I gave you life!"

Tobias linked to Selene, feeding energy into their aura, filling them with extra power.

Selene drew the fat cord in their hand toward them, fist over fist, sending a thread of their own magic back toward the Alchemist's astral form, using Tobias's energy to help reel the man in. The servitor ran and ran, binding the Alchemist like a Yule tree being roped to the roof of a car.

"You. Must. Stop. Bending. People. To. Your. Will." Selene said, every word another jerk of the rope. Every word a magical injunction.

"What do you know about *power*?"

Despite being bound so tightly he couldn't use his hands to cast, the man could still sneer. Arrogance meant he didn't know he'd already lost. Selene felt it in their bones. Arrow and Crescent and the magicians had done their work, and done it well. They could almost feel the magical sphere falling, replaced by the joy of the day.

"I could have given you so much…" he gasped. "I still can."

"No!" Tobias screamed. "Eat your words!"

The Alchemist choked, face purple, flailing in earnest now.

With one mighty yank, Selene pulled the Alchemist in and the servitor snapped the small brown cords.

The Alchemist's ætheric body shattered into one hundred pieces.

"Be you inert," Selene said, voice tolling like a bell on the astral plane. "Be your power stripped from mind and body. Be your soul diminished unto death, until you learn the lesson of life itself. That those who seek to eat the world shall eventually be eaten themselves. You are no alchemist. Your magic is stripped from your aura as flesh is stripped from bone. Be you gone! Be you gone! Be you gone. To harm. No. More."

The ragged, tattered scraps that had once been a man fluttered weakly, then, one by one, they slowly disappeared.

Until there was nothing but gray mist, and a small brown servitor. And Selene. They looked down at their palm. The red weal was fading. But they would feel the scar of it for a long, long time.

:Come: they thought at the servitor. It toddled over to them on its stumpy little legs.

:What shall you do when I free you?: Selene asked.

:Return to serve my mother,: it said. Selene saw field upon field of tobacco, clacking in the summer sun. They smelled the earthy, oily scent of it. That was good.

:Tobias?: they asked.

He shook his head. "This one's up to you."

Selene steadied themself. He was right. A witch who practiced binding must know how to unbind. Selene found the power within and, placing their hand upon the servitor's broad forehead, drew the sigil of releasing.

:Thank you.: Selene heard the small voice in their mind and watched as the servitor gathered itself together, and then it disappeared.

Selene bowed their head for a moment, and touched the moonstone at their collarbone.

:You ready?: Tobias sent.

:Ready.:

It was time to begin their journey back to their body. Their coven. Their home.

42

JOSHUA

Joshua was rapidly discovering that Arrow and Crescent coven gathered a lot. He would have preferred some time alone with Selene, but exhausted as they were, they insisted they needed the coven.

He couldn't blame Selene. If he had a group of friends this awesome, he would want to be around them, too.

So they were back at Raquel's home, this time in her fabulous backyard, sitting beneath the big maple tree, drinking fresh-made lavender lemonade. His aura still felt a bit flayed, but both Brenda and Raquel assured him he would be just fine.

The coven buzzed around, getting snacks, all except Tobias and Selene. Tobias reclined on a lounge chair, eyes closed. He looked a little too pale, and somehow thinner than before, but Joshua figured that was the by-product of the magic.

Selene, who sat nestled against him on a rocking bench, felt less substantial as well. But they still smelled of tuberoses and warm skin, edged with a scent Joshua couldn't quite identify, some combination of ozone and tobacco.

"Selene?" he murmured in their ear.

"Hmm?"

"I'd really like to kiss you. May I?"

Their head shifted on his chest, and Selene pushed back enough to look at him.

"Yes," they said, and smiled, tilting their mouth toward his.

43

SELENE

This kiss was even better than the last one. Sweet. Warm. Firm. Soft. Everything.

It smelled like lavender and tasted of summer. And the moon. And it felt like magic.

The kiss began healing a wound Selene didn't even realize they had.

They heard the coven, and Legis and Frater Louis. The rattling of ice and the scent of rosemary shortbread.

Selene's stomach rumbled and they began to laugh.

"Was the kiss that bad?" Joshua murmured in their ear.

"No," Selene replied, still laughing. "No. It was wonderful. I just realized something."

"What's that?" Tobias asked, cracking one eye open.

"You're not supposed to be listening," Selene complained.

"You're not supposed to be making out in front of me, either."

"Go back to sleep. I'll tell you when everyone else is here."

Selene and Joshua rocked together as the coven found

seats in chairs or on benches. Clearing their throat and waggling their fingers, they got everyone's attention.

"I have an announcement to make," Selene said.

"What's that, sweetie?" Raquel said.

"I'm..."

"Hey witches," Lucy said, walking through the back gate with Alejandro. He'd gone to pick her up from the hospital once they'd cleaned up the working in the park. Lucy looked fragile, slightly ethereal, but wow, it was good to see her.

Tabitha had woken up, around the time the servitor's cords had shattered the Alchemist to bits. Lucy had called Raquel, saying that medical staff were rushing around, and Tabitha's parents were crying and laughing, and Lucy really needed a ride out of there.

The Alchemist's minions had carried him out of the park. He was raving, and seemed feverish and unwell, which was no surprise. Selene had rigged the magical operation so that he could recover his faculties in time, but never do magic again. They had set the injunction, coding it into his aura with every pull of the rope.

They hadn't known they could do that sort of magic. It was knowing that the coven was taking care of the rest of it that freed them up to act at their full power.

Just as the servitor had returned to its mother, Selene had also come back home.

Lucy and Alejandro found seats.

Selene took a sip of lemonade, suddenly shy again. *The power to Dare, Selene.*

They looked around the circle, at these people they knew and loved. Who knew and loved Selene. Even Louis and Legis were people Selene was coming to trust. "I want to ask if you'll all be my family. My own family doesn't want me, so I'm choosing you."

They looked at Raquel and Brenda. Raquel's cheeks were wet.

Brenda smiled and then said, "We chose you a long time ago, Selene. *Of course* we're your family."

Joshua pulled Selene closer. That felt good. Maybe someday they'd be family together, too. Selene's mind knew that was premature, but their heart felt like it was a very good idea.

"I have fallen *so* hard for you," he whispered in their ear.

They tilted their head back until they could see his beautiful eyes.

"I'm falling for you, too."

They'd still have to take it one step at a time, but this whole being visible thing just might turn out to be okay after all.

Thanks, Moon Mother. For everything.

L ucy's palms itch and the ancestors are knocking. *Something big is about to hit Portland. Can the witches handle what's coming? Find out in By Sun.*

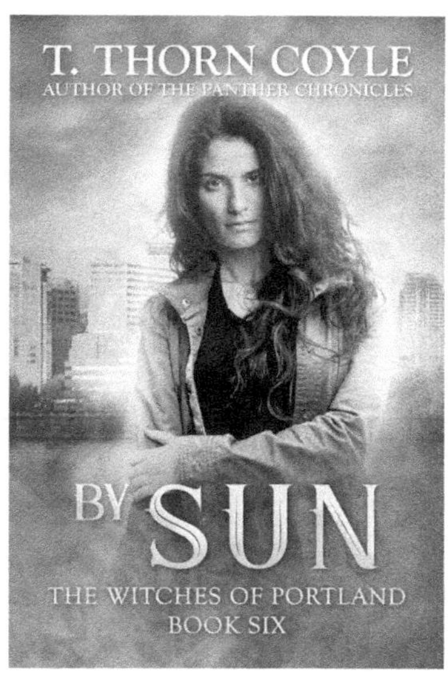

T. THORN COYLE
AUTHOR OF THE PANTHER CHRONICLES
BY SUN
THE WITCHES OF PORTLAND
BOOK SIX

*If you enjoyed this book, please consider telling a friend, or
leaving a short review at your favorite booksellers.
Many thanks!*

*Also, Thorn has a weekly newsletter at thorncoyle.com if you
want to keep in touch.*

ACKNOWLEDGMENTS

I give thanks to the cafés of my new hometown, Portland, Oregon. All you baristas are fine human beings.

Thanks also to Leslie Claire Walker, my intrepid first reader, to Dayle Dermatis, editor extraordinaire, to Lou Harper for my covers, Mala Bhattacharjee for an expert pass through, and to my writing buddies for getting me out of the house.

Speaking of house...thanks as always to Robert and Jonathan.

Big, grateful shout out to the members of the Sorcery Collective for spreading the word!

And last...

Thanks to all the activists and witches working your magic in the world. This series is for you.

ALSO BY T. THORN COYLE

FICTION

The Panther Chronicles (Complete)

To Raise a Clenched Fist to the Sky

To Wrest Our Bodies From the Fire

To Drown This Fury in the Sea

To Stand With Power on This Ground

The Witches of Portland (complete)

By Earth

By Flame

By Wind

By Sea

By Moon

By Sun

By Dusk

By Dark

By Witch's Mark

The Steel Clan Saga

We Seek No Kings

We Heed No Laws

We Bend No Knee

Seashell Cove Paranormal Mysteries

Bookshop Witch

Haunted Witch

Tarot Witch

Running Witch

Short Story Collections

A Hint of Faery

A Touch of Faery

A Spark of Magic

A Flame for Yuletide

A Hope for Winter

A Speculation of Stars

A Speculation of Hope

Risk It All: Queer Stories of Love, Suspense, And Daring

Thresholds: Queer Stories of Love, Suspense, And Daring

Non-Fiction

Evolutionary Witchcraft

Kissing the Limitless

Make Magic of Your Life

Sigil Magic for Writers, Artists & Other Creatives

Crafting a Daily Practice

ABOUT THE AUTHOR

T. Thorn Coyle worked in many strange and diverse occupations before settling in to write novels. Buy them a cup of tea and perhaps they'll tell you about it.

Author of the *Seashell Cove Paranormal Mystery* series, *The Steel Clan Saga*, *The Witches of Portland*, and *The Panther Chronicles*, Thorn's multiple non-fiction books include *Sigil Magic for Writers, Artists & Other Creatives*, and *Evolutionary Witchcraft*.

Thorn's work appears in many anthologies, magazines, and collections. They have taught magical practice in nine countries, on four continents, and in twenty-five states.

An interloper to the Pacific Northwest U.S., Thorn stalks city streets and talks to crows, squirrels, and trees.

Connect with Thorn:
www.thorncoyle.com